MW01168642

THE KISS OF LOVE

Book of Love, Book Six

Meara Platt

Copyright © 2020 Myra Platt
Text by Meara Platt
Cover by Dar Albert

Dragonblade Publishing, Inc. is an imprint of Kathryn Le Veque Novels, Inc.
P.O. Box 7968
La Verne CA 91750
ceo@dragonbladepublishing.com

Produced in the United States of America

First Edition May 2020
Print Edition

Reproduction of any kind except where it pertains to short quotes in relation to advertising or promotion is strictly prohibited.

All Rights Reserved.

The characters and events portrayed in this book are fictitious. Any similarity to real persons, living or dead, is purely coincidental and not intended by the author.

ARE YOU SIGNED UP FOR DRAGONBLADE'S BLOG?

You'll get the latest news and information on exclusive giveaways, exclusive excerpts, coming releases, sales, free books, cover reveals and more.

Check out our complete list of authors, too!

No spam, no junk. That's a promise!

Sign Up Here

www.dragonbladepublishing.com

Dearest Reader;

Thank you for your support of a small press. At Dragonblade Publishing, we strive to bring you the highest quality Historical Romance from the some of the best authors in the business. Without your support, there is no 'us', so we sincerely hope you adore these stories and find some new favorite authors along the way.

Happy Reading!

CEO, Dragonblade Publishing

Additional Dragonblade books by Author Meara Platt

The Book of Love Series
The Look of Love
The Touch of Love
The Taste of Love
The Song of Love
The Scent of Love
The Kiss of Love
The Hope of Love

Dark Gardens Series
Garden of Shadows
Garden of Light
Garden of Dragons
Garden of Destiny

The Farthingale Series
If You Wished For Me (A Novella)

Also from Meara Platt
Aislin

*** Please visit Dragonblade's website for a full list of books and authors. Sign up for Dragonblade's blog for sneak peeks, interviews, and more: ***
www.dragonbladepublishing.com

CHAPTER ONE

London, England
September 1820

THOMAS HALFORD, THE nineteenth Earl of Wycke, scion of one of the most powerful and noble families in the realm since medieval times, stared at Honey Farthingale's dainty derriere as it poked out from behind one of the intricately shaped boxwood animals in Lord Goring's topiary garden. Since it was a dark night, the clouds partially obscuring the moon and stars, he might not have noticed her hiding there if not for the lone sliver of a moonbeam shining down on her wiggling bottom and guiding him toward her like a beacon in the night.

While he stood watching, she rose from her hiding spot and tiptoed around the boxwood bear...although it might have been a dog or a kitten, he simply couldn't tell what the sculpture was meant to be. If not for the distant torchlights used to illuminate the garden paths, the garden would have been dark as pitch.

He cleared his throat. "Miss Farthingale, you are hiding from me again."

She gasped, tripped on a rock, and fell headlong into the boxwood carving. "Oh, crumpets!"

He stifled a laugh, knowing he ought to be a gentleman and help her up. But the sight of her pretty legs waving in the air was too tempting to overlook and surely required further study. She was not really in much distress and looked rather lovely sprawled within the leafy branches of what appeared to be the bear's arse. He indulged in the humor of the scene for only a moment before his chivalrous instincts flared. "May I lend assistance?"

He held out a hand and was surprised when she did not hesitate before grasping it. "Don't you dare laugh at me."

"Wouldn't dream of it." He helped her to her feet and placed his arms around her to steady her when she almost tripped over the same obstacle again.

It was the least a gentleman could do. That she felt like heaven in his arms was immaterial.

"Blasted rock," she muttered.

He arched an eyebrow. "Cursing the darkness, are we?"

She laughed softly and shook her head. "No, I'm cursing that nefarious rock."

"Are you hurt?" He was still holding her, rather liking that she was in his arms. He had no desire to release her, for she was soft and beautiful. Inhaling, he caught the light scent of summer roses on her skin.

"Not very," she said, looking up at him with those big, blue eyes of hers. Of course, it was too dark to make out anything more than their size and sparkle. But he'd seen her often enough to know their exact color. "Only a few scratches."

"Where? Let me see."

She let out a mirthful gasp. "Good heavens, no! They are not anywhere proper. Truly, no harm done other than to my dignity."

"Yes, I was admiring your delightful...dignity...when you suddenly tried to run off and took your tumble." He plucked a leaf out of her hair and another that had come to rest on her shoulder.

A leaf had also stuck to her gown just at the swell of her breast. He took it off as well, careful not to touch her as he would have liked. He was no pimple-faced schoolboy eager for a cheap, first experience with a woman's body.

Honey was not the sort of girl one trifled with in that way. Besides, he did not have a death wish. "Why are you hiding from me?"

"Am I?"

Lord, the girl was a dreadful liar. "No use denying it. I know you are. What I don't understand is the reason why. Have I said or done something to insult you? If so, I sincerely apologize."

She stood silently in his arms, to his frustration, offering no explanation for her behavior. He could wait her out. He certainly was more interested in remaining out here with her than joining Lord Goring's other guests in the nearby ballroom. Those poor souls were listening to Goring's daughter attempt to sing an Italian aria. Her voice was intolerably shrill and whiny. She could not hit the high notes. When she tried, she ended up sounding like a braying donkey.

But this was the nature of these society musicales, those horrid entertainments designed to show off the talents of eligible young women in order to lure bachelors to the altar with their siren call. Goring's daughter would do well for herself despite her voice. Her father's rank and wealth were all the siren call most men needed.

"Lord Wycke, you may release me now." Honey cleared her throat to regain his attention when he did not immediately respond to her request. Yet, her hands remained on his shoulders. Nor did she appear eager to let go of him.

"I will release you when I have my answer. Why have you been avoiding me, Miss Farthingale?"

She shivered. "Why do you care, my lord?"

There was a cool bite to the evening breeze, but he did not think the cold was the reason she was shivering. Nevertheless, he removed his jacket. "Here, put this on."

He settled it around her shoulders, then took her back in his arms. "Every unmarried young lady in London is throwing themselves in my path. I cannot take two steps without tripping over one or another of them. But you run from me as though I am harboring fleas. You have no idea the damage it has done to my manly pride. It is quite fragile, you know."

"Fragile?" She rolled her eyes. "I doubt a man who has earned the name *Wicked Wycke* ought to worry about a young nobody putting a dent in his pride. You are too full of yourself to feel any disappointment."

"You wound me." He fixed the collar of his jacket for no other reason than she looked adorable in it, and he sorely needed any excuse to touch her lovely face. "I invited you to a weekend party at my country home. You accepted and then suddenly sent your regrets. Why?"

"It has nothing to do with you."

She tried to turn away, but his hand was at her cheek, so he gently tipped her face up to meet his gaze. "Then why are you avoiding me?"

"Please, don't ask. I can't tell you."

Her voice was soft and aching, and in that moment, all his humor fled. How could he have been so stupid? He'd been treating her behavior as a little cat-and-mouse game, never once suspecting something more serious was going on.

Honey Farthingale was a quick-witted, clever girl with eyes that always sparkled and a lush mane of red-gold hair every man ached to unpin and run his fingers through. The dark red of her hair was a reflection of her spirited nature. But the girl who stood before him was one who'd had the spirit kicked out of her.

She looked achingly vulnerable and even afraid.

Not of him, he'd never done anything to scare her. "Honey..." He wasn't certain what to say to her. He rarely was at a loss for words, nor did he wish to sound glib or dismissive. "Is there anything I can do to help?"

Her mouth rounded in surprise. "Why would you want to help me?"

He supposed he was carried away by the effect of the night, the enchanting sight of her in the moon's glow, the chill to the air, and the sweet scent of flowers in the garden beds surrounding the topiary. Her scent. Even the torchlight as it flickered in the distance seemed to enhance this girl's fragile beauty.

He couldn't explain why he'd offered to help her, only that it seemed the most important thing in the world to him at the moment.

Lord Goring's daughter was no longer singing.

Thank the Graces.

The only sounds to be heard were the light gust of wind blowing through the autumn leaves, and his and Honey's steady breaths as they stood close to each other. "Why wouldn't I want to help you? Do you need my help?"

She said nothing.

"Whether or not you do, I am offering it. Are you ill? Is it a medical issue?"

Her eyes widened in surprise. "No."

He ran a hand roughly through his hair, suddenly struck by a shocking thought. "Are you..."

Blast! How could he ask if she was in the family way? But he could think of no other reason for her distress, and there was no polite way to phrase the inquiry.

He did not know why it tore him up inside. Why should he care if she'd given herself to another man? In truth, he hardly knew the girl.

But he liked her.

More than liked her, if the quickening of his heart was any indication. He did not respond this way to other women, even the ones he'd bedded. He dallied only with experienced women, those who knew how to enhance a man's pleasure. The feeling that overcame him as he held Honey was different. Better.

It surprised him, for he did not touch innocents like Honey.

Only, she might no longer be innocent. "Are you with child?"

She gasped and curled her hands into fists, obviously wishing to plant him a facer. "Are you insane?"

Relief washed over him. "Then you haven't been with a man?"

"No, I haven't *been* with any man. How could you think—"

"I didn't." He took one of her hands in his to uncurl her fist and massage it gently. When she made no protest, he took both and swallowed them up in his. He did not like that they were cold and trembling. "It was the only other reason I could think of for the desperate sadness in your eyes. Hell, I know you're innocent. It's obvious."

"It is?"

"Yes, Honey. Any man with half a brain would know at once you haven't been touched. I was afraid someone..."

"No one has. Nor will you, if that is your purpose in coming out here and pretending to care about my feelings."

He released her, angry with himself for allowing her words to wound him. Yes, he did care about her. But he hadn't come out here to steal a kiss or her virginity. Not that he'd refuse either proposition if she ever offered.

He still hadn't received a satisfactory answer to his question.

"Lord Wycke, I'm so sorry. You didn't deserve my lashing out at you just now. I haven't been myself, and I hope you'll forgive me."

She was about to hand him back his jacket, but he stilled her hand and tucked it around her shoulders once more. "As I hope you will forgive me if I've insulted you. I did not mean to cast aspersions on your good name."

She snorted.

"Why did you do that?"

"Do what?"

"Snort when I mentioned your good name." Of course, the problem had something to do with her reputation. But he'd heard of no scandal surrounding Honey. Had there been even a hint of it, Lady

Withnall, London's most feared gossip, would have gotten hold of it and spread the news far and wide by now.

She stared down at her toes. "Please go away. My name is just fine. Nothing has changed."

Indeed, she was a terrible liar. But he let her go on because she appeared to have more to say.

"I am still the daughter of a merchant. I still work in my family's perfume shops. I'm too fine for the lower classes and too low for the upper classes. I'm the same misfit I have always been."

"Is this why you've never been kissed romantically?"

"I suppose. I never gave it much thought."

He could have jumped in at that moment and offered to kiss her. Hadn't he been aching to do this very thing all summer long? And now the months had flown by, and they were standing alone in a moonlit garden.

Any rake worth his merit would have had his lips on hers by now and been working to slip the gown off her incredibly alluring body.

But he'd heard a quiet pain in her voice that left him shaken. "I invited you to my country estate for the weekend. The invitation is still open. Others in your family will be there. You'll be well chaperoned." He tipped her chin up to force her gaze to his once more. "The change of scenery will do you good."

"I don't think so."

"The countryside around Halford Grange is quite beautiful, as is the manor house itself. It's nestled in the Cotswolds, not far from Sherbourne Manor, where your cousin, Poppy, lives with her husband, the Earl of Welles." He and the earl, Nathaniel Sherbourne, had become quite good friends. "They'll be joining me this weekend. Don't you wish to spend time with Poppy?"

She nodded.

"All I own will be at your disposal. My carriage, my horses, the run of my house. If you enjoy walking, there are several lovely paths on my grounds. There are benches situated along the river where you can sit with a book. Or take a blanket and a picnic basket. If you prefer to be alone, I shall leave you alone. If you prefer my company, I am at your service."

"You sound like a travel guide trying to convince me to book a tour."

He'd won her over. He could tell by the way she was wryly smiling at him. "You needn't worry about transportation. You can ride with my mother and her companion in my carriage."

"Where will you be?"

"On my horse, riding beside you. I'm not good within the confines of a carriage. Too hot and cramped for me. But as I said, I am at your disposal. You have only to call out to me if you wish to stop along the route or have need of anything."

She eyed him curiously. "Why are you being so kind to me?"

"In truth, I have no idea. I'm not an evil man, but neither am I particularly nice or tolerant. I've earned the name Wicked Wycke. I've also been called a scoundrel, a rakehell, an irredeemable cad. I am all of those things. But I am also a good and loyal friend to those I care about."

She took his words to heart and nodded. "I could use a friend. Do you think you could be one to me?"

He cleared his throat. "No, Honey. You do not want me getting that close. My intentions toward you are…let me put it this way, friends do not have a burning desire to kiss each other."

She looked up at him, startled. "Are you suggesting you want to kiss me?"

He sighed. "Yes, and I also find myself wanting to be honest with you about it. Really, it's quite irritating."

She wasn't horrified, nor did she make any attempt to run away. "What's stopping you from kissing me now?"

"Do you want me to?"

"No."

He cast her a wry grin. "Then that's what is stopping me. I've never taken a woman against her will, nor will I start now."

"But you would be open to it if I changed my mind?"

"Mother in heaven, yes." He nodded. "As I said, burning desire."

"I don't think anyone's ever been in fiery torment over me before. Is it just me or does this feeling apply to all women in general?"

"In all honesty, I don't know. I think it's just you."

"Oh, dear. You don't seem happy about it."

He arched an eyebrow and regarded her quite grimly. "Would you be? I'm the hunter, you're the prey. So why do I have the feeling I'm the one who's about to be snared?"

CHAPTER TWO

HONEY FARTHINGALE WASN'T certain why she'd decided to accept Lord Wycke's house party invitation. Perhaps it was because he *hadn't* kissed her at Lord Goring's musicale. And now she was sorry he hadn't, because if she was going to spend the rest of her life as a spinster, shouldn't there be one moment of excitement to carry her into her dotage?

And who better to provide that excitement than Thomas Halford, the Earl of Wycke, easily one of the handsomest men in London?

The handsomest, in her opinion.

He'd come to pick her up from her Uncle John and Aunt Sophie's house on Chipping Way, where she had been staying during her come-out. Although only her aunt and uncle escorted her to the carriage, there was an entire regiment of cousins inside the house, peeking out the windows to catch a glimpse of the earl. They'd all come over earlier in the morning because they were not going to miss out on what they termed *the* event of the season.

Which was ridiculous, because she was as unimportant in society as a person could be.

Had he noticed them?

Truly, it was humiliating, so many grinning faces staring out from every room in the house. Upstairs, downstairs. She had no idea if there were more Farthingales dangling from the rooftop.

Oh, Lord, help me.

THE KISS OF LOVE

Her cousin, Lily, and her husband's sheepdog, Jasper, had just turned down the street. Lily now lived in Scotland with her husband, Ewan Cameron, but was in London to present a lecture at the Royal Society. They were staying with Ewan's grandfather, the Duke of Lotheil, at his grand London manor, Lotheil Court. The duke also happened to be chairman of the Royal Society, which explained why a society that allowed no women into its ranks was allowing a woman in as a lecturer.

Oh, no. Jasper was unleashed.

"Honey, look out!" Lily cried as Jasper gave a happy *wroolf, wroolf* and made straight for her.

There was nothing she could do as a massive, hairy weight came flying at her, landing its big paws all over her nut-brown travel outfit. Her fashionably French modiste had referred to the beautiful, golden brown color of the velvet as *noisette*, which sounded much fancier than brown and meant she could get away with charging more for it. No matter, the fabric now had paw prints all over it.

She gasped and gave a small shriek as Jasper landed heavily on her, toppling her back. She expected to take a painful tumble but surprisingly landed in Lord Wycke's strong, solid arms. She thought he'd be furious, for Jasper was now happily jumping on both of them.

Lord Wycke seemed to take it all in good nature. He was smiling as he steadied her. He put himself between her and the still leaping dog, then released her once she was secure on her feet. To her surprise, he knelt to pet Jasper and briefly play with him, not seeming to mind that he now had dog hairs all over his elegant jacket, and Jasper was licking him with his sticky, wet tongue.

Honey brushed dirt off her chic pelisse that now looked as though it had been dragged through the mud.

Lily ran over to help her. "I'm so sorry! We thought we'd finally trained him. I think he's just so excited to be back in London. Who ever heard of a sheepdog preferring the city to the Highlands?"

11

"Jasper is one of a kind," she said, trying to ignore that his thick tail was now smacking against her legs while he happily allowed Lord Wycke to dote over him.

Did he regret inviting her yet?

"Miss Honey, this might help," said the Farthingale butler, running out to her with a wet cloth in hand.

"Thank you, Pruitt." She rubbed the stains off her pelisse as best she could. The dirt came out, but she was left with a large wet spot over her right breast, where Jasper had planted one of his paws and then drooled on it. She'd had to soak it thoroughly and may as well have drawn an arrow pointing straight to her breast.

Lily let out a merry trill of laughter. "Well, my work is done here." She called to Jasper, no doubt intending to take him into the Farthingale home where he could wreak more havoc.

Honey was too embarrassed to look at Lord Wycke as she handed him the wet cloth to wipe his hands. "You can change your mind," she whispered once he'd handed the cloth to Pruitt. "I don't have to join you. It isn't too late."

He placed his hands around her waist to lift her into the carriage. "Get in, Miss Farthingale."

"Are you certain?"

"Yes," he said with a deep, gentle rumble to his voice. "My life has been far too dull lately."

He introduced her to his mother, Lady Wycke, and her companion, Dora. Whatever humiliation she was feeling melted away as the ladies greeted her warmly and had nothing but sweet remarks for Jasper, who was now rolling in the grass and then leaping in the air to entertain his audience.

Honey breathed a sigh of relief as they turned off Chipping Way and onto one of London's main thoroughfares.

Fortunately, the next few hours passed without incident.

Lord Wycke rode alongside the carriage on a handsome chestnut gelding.

She peered out the window to watch him, concentrating on him and not the two elderly women who'd fallen asleep in the seats opposite hers shortly after the well-sprung conveyance had rolled out of town and into the countryside.

He must have sensed her staring because he turned suddenly and smiled at her, one of those caught-you-looking, saucy smiles that made her feel like a rustic fool. She gasped and looked away, feeling heat rush into her cheeks now that he knew she had been gawking at him.

When she peeked again, he was still gazing in her direction. The grin was gone and in its place was a thoughtful expression. The sun shone down on the waves of his golden hair and seemed to flatter the already fine angles of his face. The ease with which he sat his horse, as though horse and rider were one, accentuated his magnificence. Even his clothes were perfection, the cut of his dark jacket in particular, molded to his broad shoulders and tapered to a trim waist.

Was it possible he looked forward to her company?

He did not appear in the least put out by this morning's scene. How could he not be? Why did he want her anywhere near him?

She wondered what was going through his mind.

Oh, she knew so little about men.

As the carriage rolled past sheep-dotted meadows and graceful trees, she glanced down at the faded red leather book in her hands. *The Book of Love*. Her newlywed sister had given it to her, insisting it would help her find the man of her dreams. Belle had found Finn Brayden and was firmly convinced this tome held magical properties.

Honey was not prone to idle fancies.

Nothing was going to fix her situation.

She had tried to hand the book back to Belle, only to find it on her bureau again the next morning. She'd then tried to return it to her cousin, Violet, who also credited this book for her happy marriage to Captain Romulus Brayden. "I've had my turn," Violet had said.

"You're the unmarried one. Stop sulking and find the man you're meant to love. If he truly loves you, he won't care about your secret. You must tell him before you marry, of course. But it won't matter to him because he'll love you more than life itself."

She sighed.

No one was going to overlook her secret shame.

Not even a meeting of the Farthingale cousins had gone according to her plans. Everyone from Rose, the eldest, to Heather, the youngest, had looked at her askance. "I would leap at the chance to marry an earl," Heather remarked to the approval of all at the meeting.

Hence their presence this morning, all of them happening to stop in for breakfast when all they really wanted to do was make sure she did not run off.

So here she was, riding to Halford Grange, and about to spend four days in the company of England's most sought-after bachelor, the Earl of Wycke.

She frowned at the red leather binding. "Fine, I'll read you."

But not in the carriage, because the jouncing would only make her eyes cross and give her a headache. No, she'd read a few chapters in bed tonight. If the weather held up, she'd take a picnic basket and read beside the river tomorrow.

The carriage halted at one of the finer coaching inns outside of Oxford.

Honey set the book aside and helped Lord Wycke escort his mother and her companion out of the carriage and into the quaint inn. His mother appeared a little confused by their surroundings. She'd been sleeping quite soundly and must not have shaken off the haze of sleep.

"May I help you, Lady Wycke?"

"Where's Tom? Where's my Tom?"

"He went ahead with Dora to arrange a private dining room for us. He'll be right back, I promise." She took gentle hold of her arm to calm her agitation and slowed her pace to accommodate the older woman as they made their way from the entry hall into the common room. The private dining rooms were located at the back.

Lady Wycke stopped and looked around in panic. "Where are we? I don't know this place."

Perhaps they'd changed the decor since she had last stopped here. Honey saw, by the way the staff hurried to attend to Lord Wycke, that the family was well known here. "We've stopped at the Four Roses Inn to stretch our legs and have a light refreshment. Would you care for tea? Or would you prefer a lemonade?"

"Tea," she said, still looking a bit confused.

"Ah, and there's your Tom. See, he's come back to fetch you."

She brightened immediately. "Tom, where have you been? I thought we'd lost you."

"Nonsense, my darling. I'm right here. Where else would I be?" He glanced at Honey.

She had expected another one of his seductive smiles, for this is how he was known as a carefree, roguish bachelor. But his expression was serious and filled with concern. He seated his mother and Dora, placed their order, and then turned to her. "There's a lovely garden in the back. Would you care to take a walk with me?"

He held out his arm to her.

She didn't wish to be rude, so she accepted. "Yes, it's a lovely day. I would enjoy being out in the sunshine."

They hadn't gone far before he turned to face her and emitted a light groan. "Thank you for what you just did."

"What did I do?"

"You were gentle with my mother." He sounded pained as he spoke. "She must have been napping in the carriage. She's been waking up confused lately."

She smiled at him. "You ought to spend more time around the Farthingales. We are all confused on a daily basis. The scene you witnessed this morning is an everyday occurrence. If that didn't frighten you off, I don't know what will."

He chuckled. "Well, thank you anyway. Not everyone would have been as kind to her."

They finished their turn in the garden and joined the older ladies for tea, cold ham, and a basket of freshly baked breads and biscuits. Lady Wycke appeared to be back to her delightful self, talking to Honey about her daughter, Anne, and her daughter's husband, Malcolm MacLauren. "What a big, handsome Scot he is. He met my daughter at Sherbourne Manor and simply swept her off her feet. He met her and proposed to her in the span of an afternoon."

Honey was shocked. "That's awfully fast."

"Indeed! Tom refused to give his consent, of course," his mother continued. "But after they'd courted for six months, and she and Malcolm remained keen on marrying, Tom gave in and agreed to their union. It is a good match. He's heir to the Earl of Caithness."

Lord Wycke said nothing but appeared decidedly uncomfortable as his mother continued. "At least Anne found her happiness. Poor Tom was not as fortunate. He—"

"Well, look at the time." He shot to his feet. "We'd better get moving if we're to make it to Halford Grange before nightfall."

The elderly ladies drifted back to sleep shortly after the carriage took off again, no doubt due to its soft rocking. At times, Honey found it hard to keep her eyes open. But she was too excited to sleep. She hadn't attended many house parties. Belle had been invited to this one as well, but now that she was married to Finn, his duties required them to remain in London.

She would be properly chaperoned by her sweet cousin, Poppy. They'd have a lovely time together, catching up on family news and keeping each other company during the festivities. Perhaps of all her cousins, Poppy was the most levelheaded. Not that any of them were foolish, but Poppy, in her own quiet way, always seemed to come up with the most sensible solutions to any problem.

Perhaps she'd confide her secret in Poppy.

She'd think about it.

"Here we are," Lord Wycke called out as they passed an open gate and started down a long drive.

Within moments, Halford Grange came into view.

Honey could not stop staring at it.

"It's beautiful," she mouthed, hoping he could read her lips. She didn't want to shout to him and startle Lady Wycke and Dora.

The manor house was breathtaking, built of stone the soft, golden color known traditionally as Cotswolds gold. The stone was unique to this region. The house was large, but at the same time, felt cozy and quite inviting. Perhaps it was the mix of elegance and rustic charm that caught her attention. The curved, almost meandering, front gardens were filled with blossoming flowers. Pinks, reds, blues, and golds. The lawn was a lush green and dotted with elegant trees.

The front door was a vibrant red that complimented the gold of the stone. The shutters were similarly painted a vibrant red.

"What do you think, Miss Farthingale?" Lord Wycke asked as he helped her down from the carriage, his hand warm and exciting as it briefly pressed against her waist.

"I feel as though I am stepping into a dream."

He was noticeably pleased by her comment, although how could anyone not fall in love with a house such as this? Perhaps he sensed she sincerely meant it, seeing the warmth of it and not the wealth it represented. "Well, that's the outside. I hope you'll like the inside just as well."

"I'm sure I will. Would you mind if I snoop about? Just the main rooms downstairs, of course. I wouldn't look around upstairs without your permission."

He laughed. "Snoop to your heart's content. It's what you Farthingales do best, is it not?"

She blushed. "Yes. We have been known to poke our nose where it doesn't belong. But only a time or two, and only for good reason."

One golden eyebrow shot up. "Good reason? Such as?"

"Crime solving, for one."

He nodded. "That is indeed a good reason, but dangerous. I hope you don't make a habit of it. Were these crimes successfully solved?"

"Yes." She began to nibble her lip, for the last crime they'd solved had led to a terrible revelation about her. She'd come here to try to forget about her situation for a few days, but it seemed it was not to be.

"Miss Farthingale...damn it...Honey," he said with surprising gentleness, taking light hold of her arm, "we'll talk later. My house-keeper, Mrs. Finch, will show you to your room. Will you meet me downstairs in half an hour? I'll take you on a tour of the house and grounds. It is more for my sake than yours. I would appreciate being in the company of someone who notices the charm of the house rather than counts up in her head the wealth it displays."

She nodded. "Yes, I'd like that."

She followed Mrs. Finch up the stairs to a lovely guestroom with a row of windows overlooking the house's rear garden. Beyond the flowers was a graceful arch of trees that ended at a meadow, and beyond the meadow was the river. She noticed her trunk in the corner by the decoratively carved wardrobe. A basket of scones and pot of tea had been set out on a side table against the wall, and beside them stood a vase filled with freshly cut autumn flowers.

"One of my girls will be up shortly to help you settle in," she said, speaking with obvious efficiency. "There's scented soaps beside the ewer and basin." She pointed toward the bellpull beside the bed. "Summon us if you need anything. More guests will arrive throughout the day and into tomorrow, so my staff may be hopping about a bit, but we'll do our best to accommodate you. I've assigned Lottie to attend you. She's a sweet, cheerful girl. I hope you enjoy your stay, Miss Farthingale."

"You've thought of everything, Mrs. Finch. It's all quite lovely." She went over to the soaps, recognizing each scent immediately since these were produced by her family.

Her sister was the fragrance expert, the one who developed their perfumes, soaps, and lotions. She was the one who took them around to the finest establishments in London, who made certain the most popular ones were always in stock, who supervised their shops in Oxford.

But she did not comment on it to Mrs. Finch, uncertain whether the woman would appreciate her being involved as deeply as she was in the family business. Being in trade was not considered fashionable. Indeed, it lowered one's standing in most circles. Sometimes, servants were the harshest judges.

Lottie scurried in just as Mrs. Finch was leaving. After bobbing a curtsy, she immediately went to Honey's trunk to take out her gowns and freshen them before placing them in the wardrobe. Honey washed her hands and face with the vanilla-scented soap since it happened to be her favorite and then changed into one of her afternoon gowns, a dark blue muslin that was more suited for outdoor excursions. She had brought along her more delicate tea gowns but hoped today would be informal.

She disliked having to change her gowns constantly, which seemed to be expected at these country parties.

Lord Wycke was waiting for her in the entry hall when she came down. "I hope you found everything to your liking, Miss Farthingale."

She smiled at him. "I did. And I must commend you on your choice of soaps. You are obviously a man of discerning taste."

He laughed. "My mother and sister only buy from your shops. Even Harrington's stocks your soaps and colognes for men. They're very good. Would you mind if we walked outdoors first? I'll show you around the house afterward."

"Yes, let's." She took a deep breath, curious to know which scent of theirs he was now wearing. *Claudius*. She recognized the hint of bergamot and sandalwood. Goodness, he smelled nice.

"Miss Farthingale, are you sniffing me?" His eyes were a deep and beautiful dark green that glistened with amusement as he stared at her.

A bolt of heat shot into her cheeks. At first, she considered denying it, but the man *was* quite discerning and would know at once she was lying to him. She was a terrible liar. She couldn't hide anything. "Yes, my lord. I'm afraid I cannot help it. Fragrances are in my blood."

He put his lips close to her neck. "What's yours. I'm afraid I'm not good at this at all. I just know it smells very nice on you."

She tried not to show how much his nearness affected her, but she also sensed he knew exactly what he was doing and purposely meant to rattle her. "It's vanilla. This is our most expensive soap." She paused a moment and blushed, realizing she should not be speaking of costs to him. But she couldn't help having a mind for business. If he didn't like it, that was his problem.

He was tossing her that affectionate smile again. "Why did you stop? I'd like to hear more."

The bounder.

Why was he being nice to her?

Well, if he wanted to learn about vanilla, she'd give him a botany lesson. "The vanilla essence comes from the flower of the orchid plant," she said as he led her into the garden, down a wide walk lined with dahlias, pansies, pinks, and hollyhocks, among others. "Right now, they only grow in Mexico, and they've proved almost impossible to transplant. But tests are being conducted on islands closer to us because the demand for this flower far outweighs the supply."

They continued to walk side by side as they conversed. He hadn't offered his arm to her, and she was relieved by it. Tingles shot through her whenever they touched, and she wasn't certain what to make of it.

However, she knew it was not a good thing.

He'd clasped his hands behind his back as they walked and talked.

She merely kept hers at her sides while she continued to chatter. "One of my favorite flowers is a variety of buttercup called love-in-a-mist. As most plants do, it has medicinal properties and also can be eaten. It tastes like pepper, but more aromatic. It isn't a popular scent, but I love its name. Love-in-a-mist," she said with a breathy sigh. "I can imagine the man of my dreams stepping out of the mist and–"

She groaned. "Nonsense, of course. But I suppose it is no secret that foolish young ladies dream of such things."

"You're blushing again, Miss Farthingale." He took her hand, but she wanted to dart back into the house. How could she have let her mind stray like this? She hardly knew Lord Wycke. Even if she'd known him for years, revealing her silly fantasies was still inappropriate.

"I'm glad you feel comfortable enough to speak honestly with me," he said, his eyes seeming wise and gentle as he regarded her. Perhaps this is what set him apart from the typical rakehells, this layer of depth she found quite appealing. "Few people ever do. My strength—and at the same time, it is my curse—is that I quickly see into a person."

"Oh."

"We all have foolish dreams, though I would not call them foolish at all. Nor are you foolish for dreaming them. Would you care to know what I see when I look at you?"

She shook her head vehemently. "No."

He appeared disappointed. "Very well, perhaps you'll change your mind later."

They walked past the flower beds and into the meadow. "Lord Wycke, would you tell me a little about yourself? I've gone on endlessly about me. I never believed I was a talkative person, but it feels so easy to chat with you. Please stop me if I get to the point of boring you to tears. I will not take offense."

He laughed. "One thing I've learned, Miss Farthingale, is that I will be placing my life in danger if I dare tell a woman I find her dull. However, you are the last woman on earth I'd ever find to be that. I noticed your cleverness at once. Well, the very first thing I noticed was…never mind. It isn't an appropriate conversation."

Since his gaze was raking over her as he spoke those last words, it wasn't hard to guess that her body was what had attracted him to her first. "Lord Wycke, don't you find it odd that we seem able to speak to each other so freely?" Perhaps it was the casual splendor of the day, the sun shining down upon the meadow. The flowers of many colors dotting the green grass. The pleasant breeze carrying the scent of the river's pure water. "We hardly know each other. It is a curious thing, isn't it?"

"It is a wonderful thing."

She nibbled her lip, not yet certain what to do about him. Her head told her to run because he had the power to make her do things she might regret and feel things she could not simply snap her fingers and unfeel.

But her heart was insisting she stay. If she wanted her kiss, he was the man to do it. The only question was when and where?

Well, there was another important question. One she had better know the answer to before she enticed him to kiss her.

What if, having experienced her first kiss, she wanted more?

CHAPTER THREE

T OM WAS RARELY one to make mistakes, but taking an innocent walk with Honey Farthingale was proving to be one of the biggest mistakes of his life. The girl was like a battering ram to his heart. Her every smile...*thwack*! Her soft laughter...*thwack*! Even the way the wind blew through her hair, causing the lustrous strands to curl becomingly around her face...yet another *thwack*!

To add to his misery, when had he ever had a conversation with a female that mentioned the words *supply* and *demand*? Or enjoyed it so much? She could have talked to him about the methods of churning butter, and he would have found her fascinating.

He groaned inwardly.

The worst part about these feelings...well, the worst part was that he was actually *feeling* something for her. He didn't know what to do about it. He wasn't used to being the one not in control of a situation. This was something frighteningly new. "Shall we turn back now?" he asked, watching her as she knelt on a rock protruding over the water and peered down to watch the fish swim by.

She was too beautiful for words.

"As you wish." She looked up at him, casting him that wholehearted smile again. There was a look of wonder in her eyes.

Perhaps it was the crystal quality of their blue that made her eyes appear to sparkle. Perhaps it was just her.

Her body was just as fascinating. The graceful way she moved.

The lushness of her breasts. The soft, slender curve of her neck. Her thoughts were pure and romantic. Charmingly sweet and innocent. His were not. He ached to get his hands on Honey.

He knew he could pleasure her, but what then?

This quandary he was in was stopping him from acting upon his desires. He simply did not know what to make of the girl.

She smiled at him again. *Thwack.* He took another slam to his chest.

"Lord Wycke, do you ever fish here?"

He nodded. "Often. Usually in the early morning. It's quiet out here at that time of day. And please, call me Tom. May I call you Honey?"

"I suppose. You've already been slipping in and out of calling me that. But we mustn't when in the company of others. It would imply an intimacy we do not share." She rose and brushed the bits of dirt off her gown. "This must be the perfect place to clear one's head of useless clutter and simply think."

"It is." He extended his arm to her. "Do you fish, Honey?"

"Yes, sometimes…Tom." She cast him an impish grin before continuing. "My father was keen on it, and I would often join him when he did. But that was quite a long time ago. Once the business began to thrive, we all had little time for anything else."

She turned pensive a moment, absently taking his offered arm as though it was the most natural thing for her to do.

It felt natural to him as well. He liked the lightness of her touch. "You are welcome to join me if you wish. I'm sure there will be others who'll take me up on the offer. We won't be alone."

She nodded. "I'd like that."

They returned to the house in companionable silence, and since she did not appear to be tired of his company yet, he continued the tour. "This is our drawing room," he said, leading her into an elegant space with a pleasant feel. His mother had decorated the place years ago.

As she declined in health, Tom began to appreciate the love she'd poured into their family home. He glanced around the familiar room, trying to see it through Honey's eyes. The chairs and sofas were pale yellow silk. But the accent pieces, namely the decorative cushions, drapes, and fire screen were of a floral design. The carpet also had flowers subtly woven in, mostly around the edges, so that one was not hit over the head with the pattern.

The larger paintings hanging on the walls were by England's leading artists, but there were several smaller ones done by his mother that he'd always thought were quite beautiful. "Who painted this?" Honey asked, stepping closer to admire one of them.

"My mother is the artist, although she hasn't been painting much lately."

"She's talented."

He nodded. "I'd like to see her start up again. She was never happier than when painting. But I don't know if it will happen this weekend."

"Perhaps if you set up her easel and supplies," she said as they walked into the next chamber, the formal dining room. "If tomorrow turns out to be as pleasant as today, why not put all of it out in the garden and see if she will pick up a brush? I am horrible at it." She shook her head and laughed. "But I'm sure some of the other young ladies would enjoy it, too."

"An excellent suggestion." He stood and watched as she glanced around the room. It was strange to watch a woman who simply enjoyed the artistry and craftsmanship that went into his possessions. He'd been watching her eyes and had yet to see that look of cold assessment as she counted up the monetary value in her head.

Perhaps Honey was just better at hiding her greed than other young ladies were. But he didn't think so. "Library next," he said when she returned to his side.

Honey gasped when she entered. "Tom, it's amazing. I think I could spend the entire weekend in here."

"Ah, now I know where to come looking for you should you fail to appear for supper."

She spent several minutes perusing his books and the few pieces of antiquity he had collected over the years. In truth, his father and grandfather had been the ones to acquire most of the artifacts. He'd only started recently.

She looked up at him when she'd finished studying an ancient manuscript that was kept under glass to protect the fragile pages from the elements. "May I ask you a personal question?"

He folded his arms over his chest. "Yes, you little snoop. However, I reserve the right not to answer."

"That's reasonable." She inhaled lightly and then blew out the breath. "Why haven't you married?"

He burst out laughing. "You might have warned me that was your question! Not answering that one. None of your business."

"I'm sorry. You're right. It was quite forward of me. It just struck me as sad—"

"Sad?" He frowned at her. Who the hell said he was sad? And what gave her the right to suggest it? "I'm having a damn good time enjoying the company of pleasant young ladies who fawn all over me and don't ask impertinent questions."

"You're taking it the wrong way. All I meant was that you are handsome, wealthy, titled, and intelligent. There isn't a woman in England who would refuse you if you offered for them. So, it strikes me as surprising that having met so many, you haven't found the right one yet."

He was still irritated with her. "It so happens, you're wrong."

Her eyes rounded in surprise. "I am?"

"I offered for the sister of the Earl of Welles."

"Nathaniel's sister? Penelope?"

He nodded.

"And she refused you? Why?"

He felt a little redeemed by her remark. Honey looked positively astounded. "I didn't love her. She fit all my requirements on paper. In truth, I didn't actually get around to formally offering for her. I had planned to and gave every indication I would."

"But you didn't?"

He shrugged. "I liked her very much, but her heart had long ago been given to Thad MacLauren, one of Nathaniel's childhood friends."

"MacLauren? And your sister also married a MacLauren."

"Thad's cousin, Malcolm. He took one look at Anne and decided she was the one for him."

That look of wonder popped into her eyes again. "Your mother mentioned it earlier. This is the most beautiful thing I've ever heard. One moment, she's sipping her tea, and in the next, she's swept off her feet by the man of her dreams. This is what I meant when I asked my snoopy question. Have you ever felt that... I'm not sure what to call it? A moment of enchantment. With so many women tossing themselves in your path, was there ever one who melted your heart?"

Yes, you.

But he wasn't about to admit it to Honey.

"It just struck me as odd that in all this time, you've never felt the magic with anyone."

He turned the question on her. "Have you?"

"No, and honestly, I don't even know what it is I'm supposed to be feeling. But I don't think it matters. I am not going to marry."

Their conversation suddenly went from amusing to something more serious when he noted the flash of vulnerability in her eyes again. But it was quickly gone, and she moved on to the next room, which was the music room.

He followed after her, shutting the door behind them once they'd entered. "We're going to talk about this."

Her chin was tipped upward in defiance when he walked to her side. "No, we're not. This is why I did not wish to come here. I'm sorry I gave in and agreed. I don't mean to insult you. It has nothing to do with you or your lovely family." She glanced around. "Or your lovely home."

"I get it. It's about you. We had this conversation in Lord Goring's garden." He held her lightly by the shoulders. She was of average height but perfectly measured to fit against him. The top of her head reached just up to his chin. She was no frail, buttercup either. She had nice curves to her body, substantial enough to put one's hands around and touch softness instead of jagged bone. "What is it about you that makes you the most unworthy debutante in England? Because I'm not an idiot, Honey. If you aren't dying of an exotic malady that leaves you looking healthy and incredibly beautiful. And you haven't been with a man—"

"I haven't!" She still had a defiant look in her eyes so that they blazed like fiery crystals.

"The war's long over. And you were probably too young to be spying for the French."

She rolled her eyes. "Not a spy."

"I believe you." He still had a light hold of her shoulders. "No, you're just a lovely, young thing who thinks no man can ever love her. Why won't you tell me the reason and let me help you?"

"Because it hurts too much." She slipped out of his grasp, threw open the music room doors, and hurried upstairs to her guest chamber.

Blast! She'd done it to him again.

He ran a hand through his hair in consternation. Was this some sort of wicked scheme? Her seemingly genuine pain and protestations of never marrying just a ruse to get him thinking of marriage?

It was not going to work on him.

And he certainly wasn't going to marry a slip of a girl by the name of Honeysuckle Farthingale. Were her parents drunk when they entered her name on the birth register? Then they did the same with Honey's younger sister, naming her Bluebell. Had they never heard of proper English names? *Elizabeth. Victoria. Eleanor. Anne.* Although not everyone was keen on naming their daughters after a queen who'd had her head chopped off. It hadn't occurred to his parents when naming his sister.

He considered going after Honey but heard a carriage pull up in front of the house and strode out to greet his newest arrivals instead. "Nathaniel. Poppy. Good to see you." He was relieved to see them, for theirs was an easy friendship, and he considered them more like family.

Nathaniel's young ward, Pip, scrambled down after them, and they all helped Nathaniel's aunt, Lady Lavinia, down the carriage steps and into the house.

Pip immediately took off to run around the grounds with Lavinia's spaniel, Periwinkle, while Lavinia was escorted upstairs by Mrs. Finch to rest in her room.

Tom, Nathaniel, and Poppy went into the drawing room to chat while the Halford footmen took their trunks upstairs. "Did Honey come with you?" Poppy asked as soon as they were seated.

His 'yes' came out as more of a grumble.

Nathaniel laughed. "What? A Farthingale plaguing you already?"

Tom turned to Poppy. "Something is troubling her, but she won't talk to me about it."

Poppy rose immediately. "You didn't try to kiss her, did you? Or invite her into your...bedchamber?"

He rolled his eyes. "No. Despite gossip to the contrary, I am not a debauched wastrel in the habit of seducing every beautiful girl I see. Nathaniel would not have let me anywhere near his sister if that were so."

Poppy left to run upstairs and greet her cousin.

Nathaniel remained seated in one of the yellow chairs, his legs casually stretched in front of him. "Tom, why are you now pacing like a caged lion?"

He stopped, realizing this is what he had been doing. "Sorry, we only arrived a short while ago ourselves, and I feel the need to stretch my legs."

"Well, that's a lie if I ever heard one. You forget, I am quite familiar with Farthingales, having been cut down at the knees by one myself. Not that I'm complaining. Marriage to Poppy agrees with me heartily."

"How's Penelope?" he asked, hoping to divert the topic.

"Deliriously happy living in Scotland. She hasn't brought Coldstream Castle down about their heads yet. Apparently, Thad can put up with her antics better than I ever could. She sends her regards to you and your family." He shifted in his chair and leaned forward. "How's your mother, Tom?"

"Not good." He ran a hand through his hair in dismay. "She still has her good days, but they are happening less and less. I thought bringing her here might help because she's always loved this place and been happiest here. She's decorated every part of it. Her touch is everywhere. But when she stepped down from the carriage, I'm not even sure she recognized where she was."

"Poppy and Honey will help you out. That's the thing about these Farthingales, they may drive you insane, but they have incredibly good hearts."

Tom laughed. "I hope so, because I'm starting to feel out of my depth. I wish Anne were here, but she and Malcolm have their hands full with their own brood."

"Have you let her know the situation?"

"Not yet. It's only gotten worse recently, and I didn't want to worry her. Just traveling down here from the Highlands will take well over a fortnight. I can't see her leaving her husband and children to come down to us when there is nothing she can do."

"Well, write to her and let her know what's going on. Leave the choice to her."

He nodded, knowing Nathaniel was right. He ought to have done it weeks ago but had been denying their mother's decline to himself. Oddly, he felt comforted knowing Poppy and Honey were here this weekend. His mother's companion, Dora, wasn't in her prime, nor had she ever been a sharp stick when younger. She was a nice woman, but never one to take matters into her own hands or ever think for herself.

Tom gave the matter no more thought as more guests began to arrive. The house bustled with activity, bags brought in and lugged upstairs, guests roaming the halls, refreshments set up to tide everyone over until supper. He'd invited several bachelor friends who'd come ahead on horseback. Their bags would arrive later by coach. They dug into his brandy upon arrival and settled in his study while awaiting their coach.

More families arrived shortly before supper, counted among them were two viscounts, a marquess, and a duke, several of them having daughters of an age to marry. He'd arranged for daily activities and entertainments for them and knew as host and as a bachelor, he'd be surrounded by these young women and their eager mothers. He hoped their attention would take his mind off Honey.

Supper was an informal affair this first evening; however, the seating arrangements remained according to rank. His mother and most of the other elderly guests had chosen to take their meals in their rooms, leaving mostly the younger crowd. Honey was seated too far from him to speak to her, but he had a good vantage point at the head of the table and could easily see what she was doing.

It bothered him that she was quiet and mostly picked at her food.

She didn't want to be here.

"Lord Wycke, your house is divine," Lady Sarah, the duke's

daughter, remarked, drawing his attention. She was a beautiful girl, lush dark hair and captivating green eyes, but there was so much *nothing* behind them. "And your title is one of the oldest in England."

Ah, no. He was mistaken. She had a head for numbers. He knew that look. She was counting up his assets. "It is. Dates back to the time of Richard the Lionheart. We somehow managed to hold on to it even during the war between the Yorkists and the Lancastrians, although it must have been a close thing with the country in constant upheaval and ever-shifting alliances."

Her eyes glazed over.

Good heavens! She didn't know what he was talking about. Had she never had a history lesson? Or come across mention of it as she studied her Debrett's?

He changed the subject. "Will you be attending Lord Forster's ball?"

"Indeed!"

Ah, parties she understood.

"It's to be *the* event of the year, I'm told. I've ordered three new gowns for it." She sighed. "I'll decide which one to wear that morning. Fashions change so quickly. I wouldn't want to be caught unprepared."

He didn't know what to say to that. If his sister had ever come home with three gowns, two of which would likely be discarded since Lord Forster's ball was the last major event of the London season before everyone disbanded to go grouse hunting up north, his father would have had a fit. He knew little about ladies' fashions other than what was all the rage one year would be woefully out of style the following.

"What else have you been doing with your time, Lady Sarah?"

She looked at him as though he'd grown two heads. "Goodness, who has time for anything? Between our afternoon social calls, visits to my modiste, dance lessons," she said with a cat-like grin, "and attending the nightly balls, routs, and musicales, who has time to think?"

"It is quite a hectic schedule."

"And one must look perfect throughout it all." She leaned closer to him and spoke softly. "I've had three offers of marriage, one from a duke. The other two were from viscounts," she said with noticeable disdain.

Was this supposed to make him jealous?

"I gather you'll accept the duke."

"Yes, of course. He's rather dull, but his home is magnificent." She glanced around, now whispering to him. "He isn't here…and you are. I'll keep myself available for you tonight."

"Won't your betrothed have something to say about it?"

"Why? I'll be unspoiled when I go to the marriage bed." She cast him a seductive smile. "There are other ways to pleasure a woman, as I'm sure you know."

She turned away from him as one of the other guests captured her attention.

So, this is what she'd spent her time learning? From her dance instructor, obviously. Her grin at the mere mention of her dance lessons gave her away. He set down his fork and drained his cup of wine.

This would have been him a few months ago, accepting these meaningless liaisons and spending the weekend indulging his urges and satisfying those of his female guests. House parties were notorious for this sort of thing.

He glanced down the table at Honey.

She was engaged in conversation with Lord Jameson. He was a friend, but a damn fortune hunter. Not that the man had a choice about it, inheriting an estate encumbered with debt and no way out other than marrying an heiress. The Farthingales were not poor by any means, but he doubted Honey's parents had the sort of wealth Niall

Jameson required to restore his earldom.

Honey was smiling at the man.

Jameson was assessing her and finding her quite to his liking.

Tom felt his blood begin to boil. He'd have to take his friend aside and have a quiet talk with him. Honey was out of bounds. No one would be hopping into bed with her. And the hell of it was, this rule extended to himself as well.

Oh, he wanted her badly.

But how could he take her when he didn't know yet what he wanted from her?

He noticed another of his friends eyeing Honey.

Bollocks.

He'd take his fists to each man, if necessary.

After supper, the women retired to the drawing room while the men stepped outside for smokes and brandy. Card tables were then set up in what also served as the music room. He wanted to partner at cards with Honey, but she was already seated with Poppy, Nathaniel, and Lord Jameson.

He wound up partnering Lady Sarah.

When the games broke up, he bid his company a good night but felt too restless to retire yet. He strolled into the garden, brandy in hand, and after a while, sank onto a wrought iron bench beside a trellis of roses.

The night was cool and the air crisp.

He breathed in the fresh scent of the surrounding trees and countryside.

There was a quiet to these wee hours, a soothing rustle to the leaves as the wind lightly swept through them. He saw the occasional firefly light up while it flitted across the flower beds. The moon shone overhead, not full as it had been on the night of Lord Goring's musicale, but on that night, it had been partially obscured by clouds. There were no clouds to hide the moon tonight. It was silvery and beautiful.

He glanced back at the house. The ladies had been given chambers overlooking this garden. He knew which one was Honey's room. A light still shone through her window, which meant she was still awake.

His breath caught when she suddenly came into view, the lamplight illuminating her splendid form as she stood peering out into the darkness.

She had changed out of her gown and now wore a thin, white nightrail. She'd undone her hair, leaving the fiery strands long and loose so that she looked like a faerie princess. When she moved, he noticed she had a book in her hand, absently clutching it as she gazed up at the moon. Perhaps she was wishing upon one of the myriad stars twinkling overhead.

What was she wishing for?

As he watched her, she wiped a hand across her cheek and then set aside her book. Was she crying?

He leaned forward when she returned to staring out the window, for he wanted to reach out and take her in his arms.

The girl was achingly beautiful.

He wanted her so badly.

But as he watched her, she began to cry again. Not heaving sobs. But her quiet tears were perhaps more devastating to watch.

Her sadness tore at his heart.

Why was she crying?

Why did he care?

CHAPTER FOUR

TOM WAS STILL watching Honey when she suddenly turned and moved away from her window. Something in the way she moved put him on alert. Something had happened to interrupt her, for she'd hastily dried her tears and disappeared from view.

He set aside his glass and hurried into the house, quietly taking the stairs two at a time.

He thought one of his friends might have attempted to enter Honey's chamber. He ran up, his blood boiling, and his hands curled into fists, for he was ready to throw punches. But what he saw hurt more than any punch he could have thrown or received in return.

His mother was standing in the hallway, wearing only her nightgown. Her hair was in disarray, and she looked utterly lost. Honey was beside her, also clad only in her nightgown since she'd run out upon hearing his mother and was obviously concerned something was wrong.

He came to an abrupt halt, feeling as though a massive storm wave had just crashed down atop him and crushed his chest. But Honey was calm and reassuring, speaking to his mother in soft, soothing words while holding her hand and stroking it gently.

This girl overwhelmed him.

He had trouble catching his breath.

He remained in the shadows, watching and marveling as this angel of mercy dealt with his mother with extraordinary patience as she attempted to lead her back to bed. But his mother suddenly grew agitated. "Tom. Where's my Tom?"

"Hush, Lady Wycke. Everyone's sleeping, and we mustn't wake them. Your Tom will be along shortly. I promise." Honey began to nibble her lip when his mother still resisted entering her quarters.

"Is he with the children? They should have been put to bed hours ago. Where is he? Is he hurt? Why won't you tell me?"

Tom took a deep breath and strode forward before she shouted and drew a crowd. "Here I am, my darling. I'm right here."

His mother's eyes lit up at once. "Oh, Tom. Where have you been?"

"Just out for a walk. Go on inside with Dora and rest now. We're to have a party tomorrow, and you want to look beautiful for it, don't you?" He kissed her lightly on the cheek and handed her over to Dora, who had just stumbled out of their room.

"Thank you, my lord. I was asleep and didn't hear her slip out. I'm so sorry. I–"

"It isn't your fault, Dora." He didn't need two agitated women on his hands. "Take her to bed now."

He stood staring at their bedchamber door as it closed.

Honey was watching him, for he felt her gaze settle over him like a soothing blanket. No horror. No disgust. But he was too overwhelmed to speak to her just yet. If he uttered a word, he'd start crying like an infant.

Somehow, she seemed to understand this quiet pain he tried to hide.

"Come inside, Tom," she whispered, taking his hand and leading him into her room. She closed the door behind them and came to his side as he sank down in one of the chairs and buried his face in his hands.

"She thinks I'm my father. His name was also Tom. She thinks he's still alive." He felt her comforting presence by his side, but he was still in too much turmoil to meet her gaze. "I'm such an idiot. I thought this party might improve her outlook, but I see now that I've made a monumental mistake. None of my guests will treat her as gently as you have. I think I'll fly into a rage and kill someone if they dare laugh at her."

"I'll watch her. Poppy will help." She sounded wistful as she continued. "I wasn't here to find myself a husband anyway. This will be the perfect reason for avoiding the daily activities you've planned for us."

He still couldn't look at her.

He'd devour this beautiful girl if he did.

Even now, she filled his senses. She had a sweet, soft lilt to her voice. It wasn't one of those ghastly, girlish voices that debutantes used when being coquettish. He hated that baby voice. It worked on most other men. He just wasn't one of them.

And her scent.

She'd washed up for the evening using the vanilla soap she'd lectured him about earlier in the day. It smelled nice on her. Subtle. Not overpowering. Perfect on her skin.

"I shouldn't be in here." He still spoke into his hands.

"I know. Don't worry. I'll make certain no one is lingering in the hall before you leave. There's no rush. I was awake, reading a book. I'll go back to reading it until you calm down. Or, I could sit beside you and listen if you have a mind to talk."

"I don't want to talk about it."

"Would you care for some tea? I had a pot brought up for me along with some lemon cake. The tea is still hot. Well, maybe just warm by now."

He finally looked at her, once again tossed upside down by her beauty. "Join me," he said, drawing up the other chair for her.

She laughed as she sat beside him. "I can't. There's only one cup. You have it. I really just wanted the cake anyway."

He watched her pour the tea and took the offered cup when she handed it to him. "I don't know how to thank you."

"None necessary. You know I did not do this to gain your favor."

"All the more reason for my gratitude." He meant it, and not in a let-me-bed-you-now way.

Yet, he had been that cad not so long ago, one to take advantage of a pretty female. It didn't matter that his guts were in a twist over the scene he'd witnessed in the hallway only moments ago. It didn't matter that Honey was too innocent and easy prey.

Of course, despite the fire she lit inside of him, he would do nothing to ruin her. He hadn't invited her here to take advantage.

He wasn't sure why he'd invited her.

Only that it felt important at the time.

Yet, there was no denying he wanted her more than ever. Everything about her overwhelmed him. Tamping down his desire for this girl was a struggle. He couldn't help it. This is what she did to him.

Were he truly a cad, he would not be above stealing a few kisses. Perhaps a little more, if she were willing. Yes, he knew just how to do it.

It would not take him long to manipulate Honey into bed.

Indeed, it would be so easy.

They were already alone in her bedchamber. She was barely clad, the light fabric of her nightrail hiding very little of her exquisite body. Her hair was tumbling becomingly down her back and over her shoulders.

She knew he was hurting and wanted to hug him.

He could sense it.

Her compassionate instincts were on fire. It would take nothing to turn her compassion to passion. But if he touched her, he would not be able to stop. Not with this girl. She affected him too deeply. "I had better go."

She nodded, perhaps eager to send him on his way because this was just too intimate. "Let me poke my head out to make sure no one's in the hall."

He let her do it, watched her sweet body as she peered out.

"It's safe," she whispered.

No, it wasn't.

He drew her into his arms and quietly nudged the door shut. "Honey…" Her name tore from the depths of his soul with a groaning ache.

"I know, Tom."

Perhaps he would have let her go if she'd pushed against him or shown the slightest discomfort about being wrapped in his embrace. But she didn't.

Instead, she put her arms around his neck and sighed as he crushed his lips to hers.

Hell and damnation, what was he doing?

HONEY HADN'T EXPECTED the opportunity to present itself on her first night here. Showed what little she knew about men. The kiss she desired and had been obsessing over how to get him to do it was happening now. Her heart was wildly leaping. She felt like a frightened hare avoiding a farmer's shotgun.

But she was not frightened of Tom. How could she be, when her dream was about to come true? The handsomest man in all of England wanted to kiss her. It was going to be magical and unforgettable.

She could see he was struggling with himself, wanting to be a gentleman and not hurt her after the good deed she'd done for his mother. Anyone would have done the same, wouldn't they? She wasn't looking for any compliment or reward.

What was Tom feeling?

His guard was obviously down, his heart in turmoil, and his body exuding pain. Was it wrong for her to comfort him? They both had need of it.

Where was the harm in a kiss?

Only one kiss, one they both desperately craved for separate reasons.

She sighed as he drew her into his arms and simply held her for a long moment, needing to absorb her against his body like a sponge taking in water. She didn't know how else to describe the way their bodies wrapped around each other.

His touch was gentle, and she realized he was waiting, giving her a few precious seconds for the chance to escape.

She hadn't the slightest intention. "Tom, I'm not going anywhere."

She closed her eyes and slid her arms up his chest and around his neck because he had a truly fine body, and she was curious how it would feel beneath her palms. *Oh, heavens.* He was hot and hard and beautifully muscled. This was better than she'd ever thought possible. Tingles shot through her as her yearning for him became an unbearable ache. Was she making a fool of herself? Did he recognize her emptiness and feel the same?

"Honey," he whispered, groaning as he captured her lips with torrid heat.

Her tingles became fiery explosions.

His touch sent her reeling so that her legs were no longer capable of holding her up. It didn't matter, Tom's mouth was on hers, warm and possessive, and he was holding her with exquisite care, as though he never wanted to let her go.

She felt safe with him.

He would not let her fall.

She wanted to cry for the beauty of his kiss and the sweetness of the way he held her. Perhaps this is how he made all women feel, but this kiss belonged to her alone, and she would not think beyond it.

This one was hers to treasure.

When he teased her lips apart with his tongue, she responded with equal ardor. She felt as though she were floating through time…perhaps floating in a timeless splendor. And yet, this moment was real. She tasted brandy on his lips, the taste of him intoxicating. She inhaled the sandalwood scent of his cologne and the male heat of his skin.

Also intoxicating.

Everything about this man demolished her defenses.

When his hands roamed along her back, she realized she wore only her nightgown. The thinnest fabric separated her body from his bare touch. She no longer cared. When he touched her neck, the glide of his fingers along her skin felt exquisite. Intimate. Intense and fiery.

She arched into him when he cupped her breast and began to swirl his thumb over it, causing its bud to harden to a taut peak.

She cried out softly in delight.

"Honey, what you do to me," he whispered, his voice hoarse and gritty as he broke off their kiss, and then she was up against the wall, cornered against it as he began to untie the lace ribbon at the front of her nightgown.

She closed her eyes to better take in the sensation of his knuckles grazing her bare skin as the ribbon slipped away to reveal what was hidden underneath.

His breath held for a long moment, almost as though he'd forgotten how to breathe. Then he released a long, ragged groan and dipped his head to one soft mound and gently suckled its taut bud. She could have stopped him any time, but she didn't want to. *Blessed Mother!* What was it about him? He had a reputation for chasing women, and yet, she'd never felt safer or more treasured with any man.

Well, he was the *only* man.

Still, she knew her heart would not respond this way to anyone else.

He swirled his tongue over her flesh, stroking and teasing as he'd done moments ago with his hand.

She was lost.

This sensation was beyond anything she'd ever imagined. She didn't want him to stop. The way he'd kissed her and was now cherishing her body, she felt as though they were losing their souls to each other.

Suddenly, he drew away.

She felt cool air against the moisture of her breast.

"Honey, I'm so sorry," he said, his breaths heavy and his voice aching. "I didn't want it to turn into this. Not with you."

"You didn't?"

She must have sounded forlorn, for he gave a laughing groan as he covered her up. "Not in the way you think. You're beautiful, of course. I want you, that must be obvious. Just not this way." His touch was gentle, and his hands were shaking as he drew her nightgown over her breasts and tied the ribbon so that she knew she had affected him as much as he'd affected her.

"What happened to us just now, Tom?" Her heart was still racing, and she could barely speak, she was so caught up in the passionate grip of these new sensations.

He took her into his arms again and caressed her cheek. "I don't quite know. Something unexpected and wonderful, I think."

"I hoped it would be like this." She emitted a shaky breath. "Is it always so?"

"No. At least, it never has been for me before. I'm not used to feeling so desperately out of control. Your heart's still racing." He laughed softly. "So's mine. Why didn't you stop me? I would have pulled away if you'd said the word. You are not a dalliance for me, Honey."

She knew it. She'd sensed it in the raw, exposed passion of his kiss and the encompassing way he'd held her.

But what was she to him?

More important, what was he becoming to her?

CHAPTER FIVE

HONEY AWOKE EARLY the following morning after a restless sleep and ran to her window to see what the day would bring. Rain? Or glorious sunshine? To her relief, the sun was out, and the mist that usually hovered low on the ground had already burned away except for a few, patchy spots.

She glanced at the red leather book on her nightstand. *The Book of Love.* "You," she said with a sigh. "Did you cause last night's…?" What would one call a kiss that led to her practically shedding her nightgown and giving her body to a handsome earl?

Tom's lips had been on her breast, and despite the years of proper upbringing, the warnings about men and their seductive ways, she had ignored it all, every last bit, and behaved like a wanton.

What was she going to do about it now?

How should she behave around him?

She had never considered experiencing more than a kiss, indeed had it all planned out in her head. *Yes, let's put our lips together. Very nice. I'm quite satisfied now. Goodbye.* But after last night, she no longer knew what to do. He was an earl, scion of one of the oldest and most respected families in the realm. No matter how much he loved her, would he accept to taint the title by offering to marry a girl who was illegitimate?

The few people who knew the circumstances surrounding her birth would never reveal her secret shame. But if matters became serious and Tom wanted to marry her? She wasn't going to lie to him. She didn't have to read that book to know a marriage built on lies was doomed to failure.

There was also the matter of her heart.

She was terrified of falling in love with him. The hurt, if he did not love her back, would be unbearable. The hurt, if he did love her back but would not marry her because of her situation, would simply shatter her.

There was no simple answer.

She'd have to think long and hard about what to do.

A soft knock at her door distracted her from further thought. "Honey, are you up yet?"

She recognized Poppy's voice and breathed a sigh of relief. "Yes, but I'm not dressed."

"May I come in?"

"Of course." She opened the door to allow her cousin in. "I was just about to ring for Lottie. Sorry, I stayed up late and was slow to get out of bed this morning."

Poppy noticed the book on her nightstand and smiled. "Oh, excellent! How far along in the reading are you?"

She shut the door behind them and walked over to the bed to give a tug on the bellpull. "I've only just started the first chapter, barely a few pages in. But I'll get through more of it today. I plan to go down by the river with the book, a blanket, and a picnic lunch. It seems a quiet spot to read and reflect."

"What about the day's entertainments? Don't you want to join in any of it? There's archery for the ladies in about an hour. Then a garden walk. After lunch, Tom said he would set out easels and paints for the ladies. I have no idea what the men plan to do. Perhaps they'll just stand around and watch us."

Honey smiled. "I'll be there for the afternoon painting. Lord Wycke hopes his mother will join in as well. Have you noticed her beautiful work all about the house?"

Poppy sank onto her bed. "I have. We've been here several times since I've been married to Nathaniel. They've visited us as well. We now have a few of her paintings at Sherbourne Manor. They're stunning, not the sort of pieces one hides up in the attic and hurriedly brings down when they come to visit."

Honey laughed and settled on the bed beside her cousin. "I think he will need our help with his mother. She isn't well."

Poppy nibbled her lip. "I know. I've seen it. You can count on me. He's a very proud man and loves his family. To see her become more scattered by the day cannot be easy for him. Not that he cares about it for himself. He'll do his duty and more as her son. It's the others he's worried about. It will kill him inside to see her made a laughingstock."

"That's it exactly." Honey nodded. "She was restless and confused last night. I heard her wandering the hall and took her safely back to her room. I don't think she'll come down before noontime. Will you watch her when she does? I'll keep an eye on her later this afternoon. If she does come down to paint, I'll set up my easel beside hers."

"And I'll make sure to set up on her other side. Sounds like a solid plan." Poppy hopped off the bed. "I'm famished. The breakfast salvers are on the buffet in the dining room. Hurry up, Honey. Join us."

With Lottie's help, she washed and dressed in an ivory morning gown embroidered with pink roses. Lottie helped her style her hair in a simple chignon at the nape of her neck and added two decorative, pink butterfly pins on either side to hold back her mass of curls. "You look lovely, Miss Honey."

The girl bobbed her head and smiled, obviously pleased with the result.

She thanked Lottie and hurried downstairs, hoping Poppy and Lavinia had not already finished eating and gone off to enjoy the day.

Unfortunately, they had.

There were no guests in the dining room when she walked in

because it was already late. Only Tom's staff was in there, working to clear away the trays of eggs, kippers, ham, boiled potatoes, sticky buns, and pudding off the buffet.

Everyone stopped in the midst of their chores at the butler's abrupt command. "Miss Farthingale, do take your time." He waved his footmen off. "May I pour you a cup of tea?"

She knew they were already overburdened and did not wish to disrupt their schedule further. Several of the older ladies in the party were seated on the veranda, chatting amiably among themselves, while the younger ladies were shooting their arrows at targets set up in the garden. "Tea would be lovely. Would you bring it out to me? I'll just make up a plate for myself and join the ladies. Please do go on with whatever you were doing."

He seemed relieved. "Thank you, Miss Farthingale."

She joined Nathaniel's aunt and several of her friends at their table. Periwinkle was seated on Lavinia's lap but hopped off and leaped onto hers the moment she sat down. She set down her plate and began to pet him playfully behind the ears. "You little cad," she teased, "it isn't me you want but my plate of food. You are an utterly shameless little beast."

Lavinia laughed heartily. "If he were a man, he'd be an unredeemable rakehell. No morals or loyalty whatsoever."

"Ah, Periwinkle," she said in jest, talking to the dog who seemed to be listening intently. "I must take great care not to fall in love with you. You are too irresistible and will break my heart." She had just finished her meal when the men and Pip came back from their morning ride. The young ladies in the archery field began to flutter and preen when some of the gentlemen came to watch them shoot their arrows.

However, Pip, Nathaniel, and Tom strode onto the veranda to join them.

The mere sight of Tom sent heat flaring into Honey's cheeks. Her entire face had to be as bright as a torch flame.

So much for hiding her feelings.

Ugh! Why couldn't she be one of those cool, sophisticated creatures who gave away nothing?

She pretended to cough, using the sudden fit of coughing as an excuse to draw her handkerchief to her lips and nose. Unfortunately, it immediately drew Tom's attention to her.

He cast her a knowing grin.

Heavens! What they'd done last night.

"Excuse me." More fake coughs. Was she fooling anyone? The only saving grace was Tom's grin seemed more affectionate than mocking. Still, she couldn't seem to gather her wits and decided her best course of action was to run into the house.

She had just darted indoors when he caught up to her. "Honey, are you all right?" He gave her cheek a light caress. "I'm not talking about your pretend coughing fit. But don't worry, I think you had the others fooled."

"Oh, Tom. What you must think of me." She felt her face burst into flames again.

"I think you're wonderful." His hand was still on her cheek, his thumb lightly stroking the line of her jaw. "I love the way you responded to me."

"You might have warned me."

His endearingly, boyish smile made her weak in the knees. "I might have, but I had no idea myself. I was no less caught up in...*that*...than you."

She looked into his eyes of warm, forest green. "Really?"

He nodded. "Which is saying something, because I'm experienced and you're not. Yet, this was a first for me. I'm not sure what it means."

"Probably nothing." She gave a casual shrug, wanting to dismiss the possibility there could be more between them. This was not a conversation she was prepared to have. Whether this feeling was for the good or the bad was immaterial.

She was too confused about him still.

"Not nothing." He drew his hand away as the sound of footsteps reached their ears. "May I get you a glass of lemonade, Miss Farthingale?"

"That would be perfect. Thank you, my lord," she replied as three young ladies bustled in from the archery field. Among them was Lady Sarah, who wasted not a moment in drawing Tom away from her.

"Your butler can fetch her the lemonade." She gave a dismissive shrug and put her arm in his. "You promised me a walk in the garden."

"Indeed, I did." He turned to the other two and held out his other arm for one of them to take. "Would you care to join us?"

"No," Lady Sarah responded before her friends had the chance. "They are going to change out of their morning gowns. It shall be just the two of us. You don't mind, do you?"

"Not at all."

Her two friends cast Honey smug looks as Tom strolled away with Lady Sarah.

Honey said nothing, merely walked to the kitchen to ask Tom's cook for a small lunch basket to be prepared for her. This was the perfect opportunity to steal away to the river and quietly read. "I'll have it ready for you in a trice, Miss Farthingale."

"Thank you, Mrs. Choate. I'll run upstairs to fetch my book in the meanwhile."

"A lovely young lady," she overheard the cook remark to the housekeeper. "Nothing like them spoiled brats who think to gain his lordship's attention."

Mrs. Finch agreed. "His lordship knows quality when he sees it. I've noticed the way he looks at her. She's special, that one."

She continued to her room but took a moment to check on Tom's mother. She was dressed and seated with Dora beside the window. It was a perfect spot to look down on all the activity. Her door was open, but Honey did not wish to step inside without permission.

Dora greeted her warmly. "Do come in, Miss Farthingale."

"Thank you. I did not mean to interrupt. How are you feeling this morning, Lady Wycke? "Very well, Honey. Don't you look pretty?" She smiled with genuine warmth. "Will you be joining the others in the garden?"

She shook her head. "No, I planned to do a little reading by the river this morning. But I will be back in time for painting this afternoon. Will you be out there with your brushes, putting us all to shame with your talent?"

Her smile wavered. "My son is keen on having me join in. I used to love to paint, but I'd hardly call myself a brilliant artist. Competent, at best. Probably not very good at it now. I haven't picked up a brush in several years."

"I'll set up my easel next to yours if you don't mind. Your paintings are so beautiful, I'd love to watch you. Even your worst will be far better than my best, I can assure you. Would you mind teaching me a little about your technique? You've mastered the art of light and shadow. In truth, I need help with all of it, the brush strokes, mixing just the right colors, bringing life to what I paint. I'm a rank beginner."

His mother laughed. "It might take more than one lesson, but it will be my pleasure."

She was heartened by Lady Wycke's response. Obviously, this was one of her good days. Honey's heart tugged. She wished they had met earlier, for this woman had a kind and gentle nature. No wonder Tom felt so protective of her. He and his sister must have been raised with wholehearted love. "Well, I'll be off now."

She leaned over and bussed her cheek, only afterward realizing it was quite forward of her. But Lady Wycke did not seem to mind and smiled back at her.

Honey managed to avoid most of the guests as she made her way down to a quiet spot by the river. She set out her blanket, placed the basket of food at one of its corners, and settled in to read her book. A giant oak provided ample shade. She heard the gentle rush of water as the current carried it downstream.

The leaves on the overhead branches rustled lightly in the breeze. She kicked off her shoes, allowing the sun to warm her toes. "Love does not come from the heart but from the brain. It is the brain that sends signals throughout the body, telling you what to feel. Therefore, to stimulate a man's arousal—"

She paused to giggle. "Therefore, to stimulate a man's arousal response, one must arouse his sense receptacles in a pleasing way. By touch, taste, sight, smell, and hearing."

Had Tom responded like this when detecting the scent of vanilla on her skin? Is this what had made him lose control last night? She certainly had lost all sense of propriety, so this clearly applied to both sexes.

What are sense receptacles?

She found the answer further down the page. "Those little parts of our body that make us tingle when we are excited about something or someone. But a man's sense receptacles do not operate in quite the same way as the female's. Nor does a man's brain."

Honey laughed. This book was not quite what she had expected, but it was interesting reading. "A man's brain functions on two levels. The low and the high. The simple and complex. When a man's brain is at its lowest function, he is only thinking of sex."

Heat shot into Honey's cheeks. "Oh, my."

There was no denying what both of them were thinking last night. Only he had the presence of mind to put a stop to it before something irreparable happened.

"It is his simple brain at work, the one formed thousands of years ago when creatures first crawled out of the primordial ooze. Very little thought occurs when the man's sexual urges are aroused. Perhaps, no thought at all. But that is good. It is evidence of his compelling need to breed heirs with any fertile female he comes across."

She snorted. "Breed heirs? Indeed."

Well, she supposed it was a good thing earls, dukes, viscounts, and other assorted noblemen felt this need. How else were their proud family lines to survive throughout the centuries?

"Love is a higher function of the brain. The important function that makes a man feel the need to protect his family. Wife and offspring. Otherwise, he'd merely spill his seed and then move on, leaving them to be eaten by wolves."

Wolves?

"But that is why man has been given a higher brain, to enable him to love. However, before he reaches that upper function of intelligence, the man must first be attracted to a mate on the simple brain level."

The only problem was, Tom was neither a simpleton nor a simple man. He was smart, thoughtful, gifted with above-average intelligence. And yet, his response last night was clearly that of a man operating on a simple brain.

A shadow fell over her as she was about to read on. Startled, she glanced up and scrambled to her feet. Her bare feet, she realized as her toes dug into the soft wool of her blanket. "You! How long have you been standing there?"

Tom had his arms crossed over his chest and an irritating grin on his lips. "A few minutes."

"How much did you hear?"

"All of it." He strode toward her and stretched his big body atop the blanket, taking up more than half of the space. He cupped his hands behind his head and settled quite comfortably on his back. He looked irritatingly relaxed. "Do you always read aloud?"

"I thought I was alone. Which I would be if you'd kindly take yourself off."

He didn't budge.

She sighed. "I thought you were walking with Lady Sarah."

"I was, but Lord Wrexham seems to have developed a *tendre* for her and was quite overset to see us walking alone. He joined us and proceeded to dutifully fawn over her. I made my apologies and escaped." He paused a moment. "You stopped in to see my mother."

"Yes." Realizing he was not going to leave anytime soon, she sank down beside him.

He noticed her stockinged toes and stared at them a moment before turning his attention toward the sky.

She was going to put on her shoes but decided not to. She was here first. He was the intruder. Well, this was his home, his grounds, his river…but she *was* here first.

"Thank you, Honey."

She nodded. "She is having a good day. She's going to teach me how to paint later. I'll be right beside her. You needn't worry. Between Dora, Poppy, and me, she'll be protected."

"I know." He paused the length of another heartbeat. "I stopped in to see her just before coming down here. She recognized me, didn't mistake me for my father. I wanted to shed tears. Imagine a grown man crying over something like that." He snorted. "But it felt good to have her back. Who knows for how long?"

"Maybe bringing her here was a good thing, after all. As you said, this is where she has her fondest memories."

"I hope so." He closed his eyes.

She didn't know if he wanted to continue their conversation, so she waited for him to say something more. She stared at her book and inhaled the fresh scent of grass and the earthier scent of the surrounding trees.

When she tipped her face up to catch the sunlight filtering through the leaves, she heard him shift beside her. "Keep reading, Honey. The book sounds interesting."

She frowned at him, for his eyes were now open and reflected his amusement. "It isn't suitable reading material."

He laughed. "Then why are you reading it? I never thought of myself as having two brain functions. But that explains last night, doesn't it?"

"I don't wish to talk about *that*."

"Fine, but neither of us is ever going to forget it happened. My lungs almost burst when I peeled the nightgown off your shoulders and saw...you. My eyeballs are still rolling in their sockets."

"May we please not speak of it? And shouldn't you be with your other guests? Won't they miss you?"

"No. Two more of my bachelor friends arrived. They'll provide sufficient entertainment. I won't be missed for at least another half hour." He cast her another of his irritatingly appealing grins. "Read on."

"You're quite irksome for an earl. You know that, don't you?"

"I'm going to kiss you if you keep stalling."

"Don't you dare! Insufferable," she muttered, but hastily picked up where she'd left off. "When a man looks at a woman, he is making a series of quick assessments regarding her ability to bear his children. Is she too old? Too young? Too sickly or frail? And while...and while a man will ultimately peruse a woman's entire body, his first gaze is on her..."

"Why have you stopped?"

He sat up and slammed his hand on the page before she was able to shut the book. "His first gaze is on her what?"

"None of your business."

He peered over her shoulder to finish the sentence. "His first gaze is on her..."

Breasts.

He had the decency not to say it aloud, but she noted the dart of his eyes to her bosom just before he burst out laughing. "How stupid of me. I should have guessed."

"You are a beast!"

"Apparently so. This explains why I wanted to devour you last night."

"I think we've read enough." She tried to shut the book again, but he wouldn't allow it. "Honey, in all seriousness, this is very interesting. What's the name of this book again?"

"*The Book of Love.*"

He chuckled. "That makes sense. It's that book Poppy, Olivia, and Penelope were carrying around that fateful summer. Nathaniel, Beast, and Thad never stood a chance, did they?"

"It's mere coincidence."

"How do you explain Romulus falling in love with your cousin, Violet? Or Finn and your sister? I know those Brayden men. They are not easy to impress. But they fell hard. Those are love matches."

"And your point?"

"Are you being purposely dense? With whom do you hope to fall in love? Or should I ask, who do you hope will fall in love with you?"

"No one. I've told you. I'm not getting married."

He leaned back on the blanket. "That nonsense again. We'll see. Go ahead, read some more."

"Or what? You'll threaten to kiss me again?"

"It isn't a threat. It's a burning desire, at least on my part. Perhaps yours, too. Do you dare deny you were in flames last night?"

"Was I? I can't recall." She opened the book to the next chapter, which spoke of the sense of sight. He'd closed his eyes again, and she thought he might have drifted to sleep after she'd read the first few pages. But he stirred the moment she paused.

"Would you like me to take over the reading?"

"No, I'll do it. I'm not about to let you get your hands on this book. Are you really paying attention to what it says?"

"Yes." He turned to face her, propping his weight on his elbow.

"I'm beginning to understand what this book is really about. It isn't so much about the senses, but about teaching us how to properly use them in order to find love. The right love. For example, the sense of sight. Too often we see what we want to see, don't we? Instead of viewing with an open mind, we force ourselves to accept whatever it is we've already decided upon. This is why most of us are taken in by magic tricks. We are easily distracted, made to pay attention to the magician's right hand while his left hand sets up the trick."

"Do you think it is this way with love?"

"I don't know. I expect it happens, but those would be instances of love gone wrong. That's the strength of this book and what it's warning us about. Take the Duke of Wellington, for example. Smartest man on the battlefield. Perhaps one of the smartest men in England. But he got himself caught in a loveless marriage. Do you know why?"

"No, but I'd love to hear the explanation." In truth, even though she was peeved with him, he seemed to be taking this book sincerely to heart and already gaining understanding from it. "Go on, Tom. I do want to know the reason why."

"He'd seen a young woman he thought was pretty, built her up in his mind to the point he believed her stunningly beautiful. He proposed to her and went off to war. When he saw her again, he couldn't believe how plain she had become. But being a man of honor, he kept his promise and married her."

"That is truly sad for both their sakes. And who's to say if she truly was plain? How could she ever compete with this goddess he'd created in his head?" Honey shook her head and sighed.

"That's precisely my point. He was not really *looking* at her." Tom shrugged. "Another man might have found her quite beautiful. Who knows? Then there are men like your uncle, John Farthingale. All it took was one glance at his wife, Sophie, and he knew he wanted to marry her. Now, after about thirty years of marriage, he still finds her to be the most exquisite woman he's ever beheld. Wrinkles, graying hair, spreading middle, none of it matters. That's real love, I think. It's hard to remain deluded for thirty years. That's a solid, healthy marriage. My parents were the same way."

"So are mine. The look of love. This is what my cousins and I always hoped we'd find."

He tucked a finger under her chin to turn her face toward him. "What happened to shatter your dreams?"

CHAPTER SIX

H ONEY SLAMMED THE book shut. "I have to go."

Tom grabbed her hand and drew her back down beside him. "No, you don't. Let's talk about what's eating at your heart. I'm stronger than you are. But you must know, I wouldn't hurt you for the world."

"But you are," she said, sounding so hopeless, he couldn't bear it. "Please, let me go. I don't want to talk about it."

"So, you're going to take Wellington's approach? Allow it to build, and in your case, allow it to fester until there's nothing left of you but a sad shell? We can face it together and fix the problem."

"There is no problem."

"Then why are your eyes tearing?" He groaned, wishing this girl did not have such a tight hold on his heart. "Gad, you're the worst liar I've ever encountered. The most beautiful, but also the worst. Fine, let's get back to that book. What do you see when you look at me?"

"I don't want to answer you." Obviously, she couldn't bear being close to him, especially as he continued to press her on the hard questions. "I want to go back to the house."

"Why? Because you're afraid of what I'm forcing you to face?" He still had hold of her hand, and although he wasn't hurting her, neither was he ready to let her go. "Here's what I see when I look at you. An angel. *My* angel."

"I most certainly am not!"

But he'd seen a flicker of hope in her eyes, and that was enough for him. He knew he was being hard on her, but whatever was haunting her, needed to come out. "Why does that scare you? You didn't find me hideous last night."

"Stop mentioning what we did...what I let you do." Her face grew hot with shame. No doubt, she was blaming herself for failing to stop what else happened beyond their kiss.

Sighing, he released her. "It wasn't my intention to upset you. But I want to read that book with you."

"Why?"

"You may not be interested in finding love, but I am. I'm almost thirty years old and need to provide heirs. You made the point earlier, that I've met hundreds of women, tripped over too many to count as they threw themselves in my way. And yet, there hasn't been a single one who's won my heart. I mean truly won it, not in a she-looks-good-on-paper way. Perhaps it's me. Perhaps these women did nothing wrong, and it's me who is flawed. If so, I had better fix the problem, hadn't I?"

"You aren't flawed."

He arched an eyebrow. "Then why aren't you tossing yourself at me?"

She blushed again. "Isn't that what I was doing last night?"

"Honey, neither of us knew what we were doing in that moment. Let's leave it at that for now." He grabbed the picnic basket his cook had packed for her. "What's in here? Enough for two?"

"That's my lunch!"

"Mrs. Choate is my cook. She's always generous with her portions." He rummaged through the basket. Cheese. Bread. Apples. Roast goose. "A feast fit for a king. See, there's plenty for the both of us. Aren't you thrilled?"

She rolled her eyes. "I'm in raptures."

He laughed. "You ought to be. I'm *the* bachelor every young lady in London society is hoping to capture. But no more talk about that. I see we have visitors coming our way."

She turned to follow his gaze, then turned back to him and shook her head merrily. "Pip and Periwinkle. Better hide the food, or there'll be none of it left for us."

He tucked the goose back into the basket and shut the lid just as the little spaniel reached their blanket and immediately began to sniff everywhere. He sniffed Tom's boots. He sniffed the basket. Then he sniffed Honey's toes since she hadn't put on her shoes. After that, he climbed on her lap and sniffed.

She nudged him off her lap and shot to her feet. "Periwinkle! Bad dog!"

Tom stifled the urge to laugh. Ah, Periwinkle was definitely male. The little rake had dug his nose where it didn't belong. Honey's face was once again in flames. That innocence about her simply enchanted him.

She had a rare honesty of feeling. A generous, loving heart. No guile. No deception. No scheming motives. Perhaps this is why he was so drawn to her.

She was quality.

He'd be a fool to let her slip away.

Not that he was thinking beyond merely getting to know her better. He'd given his sister and her husband a hell of a time when they'd met and fallen instantly in love. He'd demanded they wait six months. He would do no less.

He wasn't the rash sort who would propose to a girl within a weekend of getting to know her. Besides, Honey had her *secret*. He needed to find out what it was before opening his heart to her.

After the three of them and their gluttonous companion had shared the food in Honey's picnic basket, she tugged on her boots and ran around with Pip and Periwinkle, tossing a pine cone and cheering as both boy and dog ran to fetch it. Well, Pip was a growing boy and could run around for hours without exhausting himself. Periwinkle was the most spoiled animal Tom had ever encountered. The pampered rascal would likely expect Pip to carry him back to the manor house once he was spent.

Tom participated in the silliness and couldn't recall when he'd had a nicer time.

He knew he'd overstayed his visit and did not want others coming down here to look for him. He returned to the blanket to grab the picnic basket and carry it back to the house since it was heavy, and he didn't want Honey lugging it back on her own.

How had she carried it down here while it was full of food? The basket was almost as big as she was. He hauled it onto his shoulder.

He glanced at the book still lying on the blanket, its leather binding faded and worn. A strange feeling suddenly came over him. He needed to finish reading it with Honey. He didn't know why it was suddenly so important but sensed her happiness depended on their getting through it together. His, too, if he wanted to be honest about it.

He wasn't sure if they'd have the chance before the weekend was over.

Perhaps he was being ridiculous.

Yet, the tug of that book felt real.

More disquieting, it seemed to draw raw feeling out of him. Feelings of possessiveness. Desire. Hunger. Protectiveness. Yes, that one was quite overwhelming, the need to protect Honey. But from what?

He had to get answers out of her. How? Perhaps this book was the way. He stared at it, almost feeling it throb with life. What was this book trying to tell him? That her happiness was intertwined with his?

He knew it.

He felt it.

But Honey was resisting with all her might.

She returned to his side once Pip and Periwinkle left her to go back to the house. Her cheeks were a delicate pink, and her eyes were a sparkling blue. He tried not to gape at her heaving chest, but it was hard to overlook.

Yes, her endowments were spectacular.

He forced himself to turn away before he made a leering arse of himself. When he turned back, he noticed a few soft curls had blown out of place. He set the basket aside and reached out to brush them back behind her ears. She had beautiful hair, the color of a fiery sunset. The butterfly pins she used to hold the strands in place were simple and charming. They suited her.

There was just something about this girl.

He wanted to kiss her again.

But when did he not?

"I had better go back as well," he said, clearing his throat and picking up the basket again. "My guests will certainly be looking for me by now. I'd rather they not find us together."

"I understand."

He met her gaze. "Do you? It's simply that I don't like everyone knowing my business. I like my privacy, but I have so very little of it. I enjoyed my time with you, Honey."

Her lips were tightly pursed, as though she wanted to chide him for forcing her to face this mysterious thing haunting her. But she sighed and smiled at him. "For the most part, so did I."

"Good." He looked down on her. "I meant what I said. I want us to read this book together. Promise me that we will. It's important we do."

"How? Your absence will be noticed. Guests will come looking for you. I'm surprised they haven't already. I don't want them finding us and asking questions about the book."

"I could come to your bedchamber quietly tonight."

She gasped and curled her hands into fists. "Are you mad?"

"Yes, I must be. But I give you my word of honor. Nothing like last night shall happen again. We'll read. Just read."

"Just read?"

"Upon my oath."

She snorted but did not outright refuse him.

That had to count for something. He had hours until evening. He'd give her time to contemplate her answer. "I'll carry the basket back to the house." He already had it on his shoulder.

She nodded. "Thank you. I'll follow a few minutes after you. As you said, better that we not be seen together."

The hours dragged for him after he left Honey, although he was occupied with the other young ladies who fluttered around him. Lady Sarah was back and looking as though her ardent suitor Wrexham was simply a bore. Too bad. She was hard to handle. Surely one of his other friends would be glad to occupy her time, especially at night, which is what she seemed to desire of him.

He made certain to remain close by when the easels were set up for the ladies in the garden. Honey was true to her word, as he knew she would be. She'd taken the easel closest to his mother's and made certain Poppy took the one on her opposite side. He'd seen enough of his mother's behavior to know when she was alert and when she was becoming scattered. He was worried. She seemed to be teetering on the edge right now.

But he was surrounded by other guests demanding his attention and thought it best to step away and leave matters to Dora and the Farthingales. One of them would summon him if things got out of hand. He trusted Honey and Poppy especially. Smart ladies. Sensible.

Unlike the peahens now surrounding him.

Lady Sarah and her friends had accosted him again, tossing inane questions at him. He remained chatting with them, purposely moving them away from where his mother had set her easel. "What will you be painting?" he asked Lady Sarah, hoping to distract her attention as she dipped her brush in a pot of paint.

He knew this breed of debutantes quite well, for their ilk never changed from season to season. They were the beautiful daughters of wealthy lords, pampered since birth, and not above belittling others to enhance their standing. They bullied and humiliated, all the while keeping their eyes on the prize they hoped to achieve. A duke, marquess, or earl.

Lady Sarah would never settle for anything less, and she fully intended to marry her dull duke and make him a cuckold within a month of their marriage. Her witless companions, Lady Amelia and Lady Jenna, took their guidance from her. They weren't quite as clever or beautiful as Sarah, but their family wealth would gain them equally impressive titles. "And you?" he asked said witless companions as they dipped their brushes into their pots.

"We could draw you," Lady Sarah remarked, tossing him another of her practiced, seductive smiles that he found about as alluring as moldy cheese. "Would you take off your clothes for us?"

Her friends were shocked and giggled.

"And bare my arse to the world? Not remotely tempting."

She sidled up to him. "Perhaps later then, when no one else is watching? If you're shy, we'll take off our clothes as well."

"Sarah! You are shameless," Amelia said but eyed him avariciously. By her cat-like grin, he knew that she'd go along with the ridiculous proposition.

It was possible he was turning into a prig, for he would have enjoyed such games only a few years ago. He thought briefly about what Honey had read to him out of her book. What did he see when he looked at Lady Sarah?

She was considered a beauty, but there was an ugliness to her character that he could not overlook.

He left them to their painting and took his time wandering among the other ladies. The rest of them were quite pleasant. Some of them intended to sketch flowers and others attempted to draw the manor house. Lavinia decided to draw Periwinkle.

He smiled, no surprise there.

Poppy had decided to paint a portrait of Pip. He suspected it was a ruse to keep her eyes on the boy and keep him out of mischief. Pip was delighted when several other ladies politely asked if they could draw him, too. Of course, there were none of the lewd overtones he'd received when speaking to Lady Sarah and her friends.

Those three needed close watching to keep them out of mischief.

Well, Sarah's father was the Duke of Remson, a widower. He'd brought his daughter and her friends to the party and was obviously unprepared to deal with them now that they were old enough to enter society. Tom would have a quiet word with him if they got out of hand.

As the ladies settled in to paint, he sauntered over to his mother's easel and peered over her shoulder. He was curious to see what she was drawing on her canvas.

"Bloody hell," he muttered under his breath, turning to glance at Honey in dismay.

She cast him a sympathetic smile in return. "It's all right, my lord."

No, it wasn't. His heart sank, for his mother had yet to place a drop of paint on the canvas.

Honey set down her paintbrush and joined him beside his mother. "Lady Wycke, why don't you draw something nice for your son? What do you think he might like?"

"Oh, Tom always loved his horses."

"I noticed his beautiful chestnut gelding. He rode it here from London. Would you like to draw his horse? I shall try to do the same, and we shall compare."

His mother cast her a hesitant smile. "Yes, that's a lovely sugges-tion. Chestnut, you say. I'll have to mix my paints. Oh, dear. Will I have time to finish it?"

Honey took the lid off one of her pots. "We'll pick it up again tomorrow if we need to."

Tom placed a comforting hand on her shoulder. "You have the entire weekend, my darling. There's no rush. Take all the time you need."

The distant shrieks and derisive laughter coming from Lady Sarah and her friends startled his mother. She immediately lost her concentration and became agitated. Honey took hold of her hand. "I think a butterfly must have landed on her nose."

His mother laughed and appeared to calm down, but the blasted peahens shrieked again.

Poppy now came over. "Lady Wycke, I've started to draw Pip. Come have a look? What do you think? Isn't he a handsome, young fellow?"

To Tom's relief, Pip struck a pose, first appearing quite serious, then making funny faces that had all the ladies laughing, including his mother. When she turned back to her canvas, she'd forgotten what they'd agreed to draw.

Honey still had hold of her hand. "It's quite all right, Lady Wycke. Perhaps something simpler might be better."

"Yes. Simpler."

Once certain his mother had calmed, Tom left them to join Nathaniel in his study for a few minutes. He thought it would be safe enough. Some of the bachelors he'd invited were now standing beside Lady Sarah and her friends, occupying their attention. He expected the conversation to be bawdy if the leers on the men's faces were any indication. He didn't care. So long as they kept Sarah and her peahens occupied and away from him.

He strode into the study and poured himself a brandy.

"She's going to be trouble," Nathaniel said, peering out the window toward them. "Lady Sarah, I mean. She's been trying to gain your notice and is frustrated that you're not interested. To her, you're the ungettable get, if you know what I mean."

Tom joined him by the window. "I know. She likes a challenge.

The more I resist, the more determined she is to lure me into her bed. I feel sorry for her donkey of a duke."

"Don't be. I'm sure he'll keep a mistress in town. The beautiful wife is just for show. Also, he'll now be connected to her father by marriage. I doubt he'll care what she does, so long as she's discreet about it."

Tom drank a little of his brandy, enjoying its smooth heat as it slid down his throat. "Hah! That girl does not know the meaning of discretion. She's poison. I wish I could confine her to her quarters for the next few days. My mother invited them. She and the late duchess were very good friends. I wish I had struck them from the guest list. Too late now. Needless to say, they won't ever be invited here again."

Nathaniel kept his gaze on the outdoors as he spoke. "Lavinia was close friends with the duchess, too. Well, it's done."

"Right. Let's hope she does nothing more to overset my mother." He finished his brandy and set the empty glass down on his desk. "I'd better get out there and see how Honey and Poppy are managing."

Nathaniel set down his glass as well. "I'll go with you. I'm curious to see what Poppy decided to paint."

Tom laughed. "She's doing a portrait of Pip."

"And the boy is sitting quietly for her?" Nathaniel arched an eyebrow and grinned. "She's far smarter than I am. Killing two birds with one stone. Getting her painting done while keeping watch over my wayward ward. She keeps all of us in line with such finesse. I am in awe of her abilities."

When they reached his mother and saw that she still had not put a brush to her canvas, Tom's heart sank. He felt Nathaniel's hand on his shoulder, knowing his friend was trying to calm him. He didn't bother to deny it, for his heart was in his throat, and his hands were clenched. He wanted to pick up her brushes and hurl them into the river.

He wanted to smash his fist through her empty canvas.

If he weren't in company and needing to keep his wits about him, he would have done just that. He also would have grabbed a bottle of brandy and shut himself in his study to drink himself into a stupor. He wanted to find oblivion, to numb himself from the pain of watching her bright light dim to nothing.

"Getting angry won't solve anything," Honey said in a whisper, obviously sensing he was about to erupt.

"I still want to hit something." He noticed her frown and sighed. "I won't. You needn't worry."

The other ladies had finished their works of art. Lady Sarah and her friends were now heading toward them. He glanced at the untouched canvas and knew he did not want that mercenary shrew to see it. While he doubted those three would ever dare to utter a cruel remark to his mother's face, they'd have a good jest about it behind her back.

This is what he'd feared most.

He was about to step forward to steer them away when Honey took matters into her own hands. She quietly switched her canvas with his mother's empty one. Lord, he knew what she was doing and wanted to kiss her for it. Of course, he'd made her that damn promise not to touch her while they read that book together. Then again, he'd only promised not to touch her while they were in her bedchamber.

He wouldn't be breaking any oaths if he kissed her elsewhere.

And he was going to kiss her, that was not in doubt.

But now was not the time to be thinking of such things. He gave her hand a quick, light squeeze. "You don't have to do this."

"Yes, I do. Let them make fun of me. I can take it. And I don't give a fig what they think of me."

Standing beside her and not being able to show his appreciation was something he found surprisingly difficult. He wanted to tell her all that was in his heart, spill his bloody guts to her. But she seemed to sense his gratitude and everything else he was feeling. She gave his hand a light graze in return. "It'll be all right, Tom."

As expected, Lady Sarah put on a show for her friends. "Lady Wycke, you've drawn such a lovely rose."

His mother simply smiled.

Tom could see she was beginning to slip away, but Lady Sarah was too busy preparing to cause trouble elsewhere to notice. "Roses were always your favorite," Tom remarked, moving between his mother and this shrew.

He happened to glance at the painting and was caught by surprise. Honey had some talent herself.

"Why Miss Farthingale, you've drawn nothing. Do you think yourself too far above us to participate in Lord Wycke's entertainments? Or perhaps he has private entertainments reserved just for you."

He sensed Honey was about to hurl back a retort and now purposely stepped in front of her to prevent the situation from spinning out of control. This was his house. His party. His duty to protect her. "Lady Sarah, I suggest you curb your spiteful tongue. If you insult any of my guests again, I shall toss you out on your ear."

"How dare you–"

"Will you put it to the test?" He crossed his arms over his chest. "I promise you, I will not indulge your pettiness."

"Let's go, Sarah," Lady Jenna said, reaching out to draw her away.

"Fine, have it your way." She turned in a huff, knocking over Honey's easel and paints. She offered profuse apologies when some of the paint spilled onto Honey's gown, but Tom had seen her sly, malicious smile and knew she'd done it on purpose.

"That does it." He was livid.

He took a step toward her, taking no pains to hide his wrath. But Sarah and her friends fled like frightened rabbits. He'd hunt them down later. Right now, he was more concerned about Honey.

He'd talk to Sarah's father later and ask him to make up an excuse to take her away.

Nathaniel once again placed a hand on his shoulder. "She's inconsequential. Tend to your mother. She's getting upset."

Honey and Poppy were already on the task, leading her upstairs under the guise of needing her to summon Mrs. Finch to Honey's room. He and Nathaniel remained with their other guests, pretending all was sunshine and flowers when nothing could be further from the truth. To his relief, young Pip came to their rescue, diverting everyone's attention by summoning Periwinkle off Lavinia's lap and showing everyone the tricks he'd taught the pampered dog.

Periwinkle knew how to turn on the charm as well, and soon everyone was watching his little show, clapping and laughing. Tom took advantage of their distraction to run upstairs and see that everyone was all right.

Dora and Poppy were in his mother's quarters, calmly tending to her. She seemed fine, no longer agitated, probably not remembering what had happened only moments ago. Since they did not require his assistance, he retreated into the hall and walked next door to Honey's chamber.

Her door was shut, and he heard no sounds coming from inside. He knocked lightly. "Miss Farthingale, is there anything I can do for you?"

No answer.

He knocked louder.

Still no response.

Where could she be?

Of course, she hadn't wanted to track paint all over his house. She must have gone to his kitchen seeking help to remove the stains. He hurried down there and found her seated in a corner. She'd removed her gown and was bundled up in one of his sister's old robes while her maid and Mrs. Finch attempted to restore her gown.

By the frown on his housekeeper's face, he knew it was too far gone to salvage.

Honey cast him a wry smile as he approached, his eyes only for her, and ignoring the stir he was causing by appearing in the kitchen. "Miss Farthingale, you need only provide me the name of your modiste, and I'll send word to her at once to make you a duplicate. You looked particularly lovely in that gown. I'm so sorry it is ruined."

"Thank you, my lord. You are too kind."

"Is there anything else you need?" He wanted to draw up a chair and simply wait down here with her but knew it would cause tongues to wag. Instead, he knelt beside her, prepared to leave in a moment before others made more of his presence here than merely polite concern.

He didn't care for himself but wanted no whispers about Honey. He'd been the object of fascination and scandal for most of his life. He'd given the gossips plenty of fodder and was used to the nasty chatter that would circulate until the next scandal broke, and his misbehavior was forgotten.

Honey wasn't used to such treatment. It was not something a young woman could easily escape. Naughty behavior was considered *manly* in a man, but unforgivable in a woman.

She smiled at him. "Your staff is taking excellent care of me. I'll let them know if I desire anything."

"Very well, I'll leave you in their capable hands." He rose and turned to walk away, overlooking the sudden bustle of activity as Mrs. Choate and her scullery girls, as well as every footman and maid down here, pretended they hadn't been shirking their duties and listening to every word spoken between him and Honey.

He returned to their other guests. Lady Sarah and her friends were missing, but so were several of the bachelors, among them a few who had enough sense to think for themselves and keep those silly debutantes out of mischief.

Lady Sarah's father was chatting with Lavinia, obviously unaware of his daughter's antics. He decided to take the duke aside later this evening and have a quiet talk with him.

He didn't care about these frivolous girls.

His thoughts were all on Honey.

He'd given his oath he wouldn't touch her while they read the book in her bedchamber. He'd given his oath and meant to stand by it no matter how desperately he wished to take her in his arms and kiss her. Still, it would be a mistake to be alone with her. There would be no getting out of the scandal if they were found out.

He'd offer to marry her, of course.

It would be no hardship for him.

He was long beyond sowing his wild oats and was ready to settle down. The more time he spent with Honey, the more certain he was he'd found the one.

Of course, he'd catch no end of hell from his sister. Even he ought to be kicking himself for his rash behavior. Two days. Of course, he'd been observing her for months. But eyeing someone from a distance hardly counted. Was he ready to marry this girl only upon two days' acquaintance?

Hadn't he been warning himself to take it slow?

His heart didn't seem to care.

He'd made Anne wait six months.

He now understood the torment he'd put her through.

He'd apologize the next time he saw her.

Of course, there remained the problem of Honey's secret. He still did not understand why she wished to remain unmarried.

But if the choice were taken from her? Not that he would ever stoop to such a thing, but if they were caught together and it was either marry him or be forever ruined?

Would she accept his offer of marriage?

To his dismay, he wasn't certain she would. So, the question remained. What secret shame was she hiding from him?

CHAPTER SEVEN

HONEY KNEW THERE would be trouble from Lady Sarah and her cohorts, Lady Amelia and Lady Jenna. Unfortunately, she didn't know where or when they'd put their mean-spirited schemes into action. She had no doubt they were plotting something. They had been casting her sly glances throughout supper and were now smiling smugly as everyone walked to the music room for this evening's entertainment. It was to be a music recital, and all the young ladies would take a turn to sing or play a tune on the pianoforte.

Whoever had thought up this torture?

The men, if they were anything like those in her family, would find any excuse to hide until it was over. But since they had nowhere to run, she supposed most had already numbed themselves by drinking heavily at supper and during their after-supper smokes.

"Are you ready?" Poppy asked, taking the seat beside her.

"Yes, I can't wait to get it over with." Since Poppy was married, she no longer needed to be put on display. But they often gave recitals together during family events, so they'd arranged to sing a duet of one of their favorite country tunes.

"It won't be so bad. We'll get through it. Too bad my sister isn't here. She'd show up those peahens."

"Indeed, Violet would put them to shame." No one had a lovelier voice than Poppy's sister. But she wasn't here, so they'd have to put those pampered debutantes to shame on their own. Their voices were fairly good. They would not embarrass themselves.

When their turn came, they walked up to the pianoforte, feeling quite relaxed. They'd performed this tune many times before, although to a family audience. But it was a pleasant, lively lilt, and the two of them knew how to put the song over. In no time, they had their audience joining in and clapping along with them.

Lady Wycke was seated in the front row with Dora, Lavinia, and Pip. Of course, Periwinkle was perched on Lavinia's lap, his tail wagging and tongue dangling as he yipped along with the tune.

Honey was pleased to see them all participating and obviously enjoying themselves. Tom and Nathaniel were standing off to the side. When she spared a glance at Tom, she thought her heart would melt.

The smile he cast her was so loving and intimate.

It felt as though their souls knew each other.

Words weren't necessary to convey the pride, happiness, appreciation, and so much more he was feeling in that one smile.

Lady Jenna bumped into her shoulder as they passed each other when exchanging places. It was Jenna's turn to sing, and Honey felt a twinge of satisfaction knowing the girl's recital would not be nearly as well-received as hers had been.

But it worried her that these three had grown so bold as to openly intimidate her. Lady Amelia had bumped into her on their way into the dining room earlier. Those little shoves were nothing. It was what would come next that had her worried.

She needed to make Tom aware of her concerns, but she couldn't do it now. She'd have to climb over others to get to him. It would simply have to wait until the musicale was over. However, he was keenly aware of all that was going on and very little escaped his notice. He'd probably seen Lady Sarah's friends bump into her as they passed.

She'd leave it to him to deal with them.

After the last debutante sang, the onlookers gave them all a hearty round of applause before making their way to the drawing room where the card tables had been set up. Ordinarily, the music room would have been used for this purpose, but the recital took precedence this evening.

Several families came over to congratulate her on her performance. Some of the other young ladies came over as well, offering their sincere compliments.

Truly, were it not for Lady Sarah and her toadies, she would be having a lovely time.

She meant to go over and join Lady Wycke's foursome for whist, but Lavinia, Poppy, and Nathaniel had already taken charge. She was about to quietly slip away when Tom came up behind her and took her arm. "Come join my table. We need a fourth."

He didn't give her the opportunity to refuse before leading her across the room. "You know Lord Jameson," he said, since they'd been introduced earlier. "And have you met his cousin, Lady Phillipa?"

She smiled at the pretty brunette. "Yes, we met at supper last night. I saw you won the archery prize. Well done."

Phillipa laughed. "Thank you. And your recital was so much fun. You have a lovely voice."

Tom held out a seat for her at his table. "I've always suspected women were far more accomplished than we simple men. You ladies have proved it. What do you say to ladies against the gentlemen? What do you think, Jameson? Can your fragile pride take the loss?"

His friend laughed. "Phillipa has been running circles around me for years. I'm quite used to losing to her."

The men won the first game, but she and Phillipa won the second. The hour was getting late, and many of the older guests had retired to their chambers. Tom's mother had gone up about half an hour ago, escorted by Nathaniel and Poppy.

"Shall we play a third?" Jameson suggested.

Tom glanced around. "No. Let's leave it as all even. Seems most everyone has finished their card games, and different games are about to start."

Jameson nodded. "Bad lot, those three."

Tom cast him a grim glance. "You noticed."

He and Phillipa nodded. "Hard to overlook. Miss Farthingale, they seem to have taken a dislike to you. My cousin and I will do our best to keep an eye on them, but they're up to something."

Tom rose. "I know. I meant to talk to Lady Sarah's father this evening, but he turned in early complaining of a headache. I'd better go see what she's up to. Would you two mind escorting Miss Farthingale upstairs?"

Phillipa rose as well. "Not at all. Come along, Miss Farthingale. My cousin and I will see you safely back to your quarters. I almost hope we encounter Lady Sarah in the hall. I wouldn't be averse to poking that girl in the nose...or shooting her in the backside with one of my arrows."

Honey laughed. "She does bring out the best in everyone, doesn't she? I was plotting to toss water balloons at her head."

"Far too gentle. I would have filled them with paint and hurled them at her. I saw what she did to your lovely gown. What a pity. Is there any chance it can be salvaged?"

"No, unfortunately." They continued to chat as they climbed the stairs and started down the hall, their conversation now about tomorrow's activities. "Lord Wycke has invited me to go fishing in the morning. I gather he's put together a small party of avid anglers. Will either of you be going?"

Lord Jameson shook his head. "Not me. Too early. Too much sunshine and fresh air," he jested. "It isn't good for my dissolute constitution."

Phillipa poked him in the ribs. "You're not nearly as bad as you make yourself out to be. But I will admit, you can be heartily irritating at times." She turned to Honey. "I won't be there either. Too quiet a sport for me. I'll see if anyone is interested in a rousing game of shuttlecock."

Honey bid them good evening, but as she went to open her door, she saw that it was already open.

"What's wrong?" Lord Jameson asked.

She frowned. "I'm sure I closed it earlier."

"Perhaps your maid came in to turn down your bed and scurried out to tend to something else," Phillipa suggested.

"Yes, it could be." But the little hairs on the back of her neck began to prickle. "Will you stay with me a moment?"

They both nodded.

She entered, lit the lamp on her bureau, and immediately went to her wardrobe to open it and peer in. Next, she peered under her bed. No one was lurking in either of those places. She checked behind her drapes and then behind the door.

"Do you think someone broke in here, Miss Farthingale?" Lord Jameson asked.

"I don't know. I have an odd feeling..." Something felt wrong, but she couldn't figure out what it was. Nothing seemed to be out of place.

She opened her drawers to check if any of her jewelry was missing, but she didn't have anything all that expensive, and every necklace, bracelet, pin, and set of earrings seemed to be exactly where she'd left them. She had nothing else of value. No one was going to steal her shoes or undergarments.

She opened up the wardrobe again and sighed. "Everything seems to be in order. I think Lady Sarah just has me on edge."

Neither of her companions was smiling. "Lock your door," Phillipa cautioned.

"I will."

Lord Jameson glanced down the hall. "I'll make sure no one's lurking about. Will you be all right?"

She smiled at him. "Yes, I'm sure I will be. I'm sorry I alarmed you."

"Not at all." Phillipa bussed her cheek. "Goodnight, Miss Farthingale. We'll see you tomorrow."

Once they'd left, she locked her door and fell onto her bed with a groan. "Ugh!" She was letting that horrid debutante get to her. The hour was late, and she did not wish to disturb poor Lottie, who must have gone to bed hours ago. She slipped out of her gown and corset, then donned her nightgown and robe.

After washing her face and hands, she decided to read in bed. Tom had asked her to wait for him so they might read *The Book of Love* together. She needed something to occupy her mind. It wasn't cheating, really. Nor was it breaking a promise since she hadn't given him one. Besides, she doubted he'd come to her chamber tonight, even though he'd said he would.

They'd had a long day, and he needed to remain alert and well-rested for whatever mischief Lady Sarah and her friends were planning tomorrow.

As for herself, she wouldn't manage more than a few pages before dozing off.

She absentmindedly reached for the book she'd left in the drawer of her nightstand. It wasn't there. "Oh, no!" This is what the little witch had taken! But how was she to prove it? "No, no." She had to stay calm. Perhaps Lottie had tucked it away elsewhere.

A search of all her drawers turned up nothing.

Her heart was now beating erratically.

She had to find the book.

Was it possible Tom had taken it? She didn't think so, but she'd ask him first.

She quietly knocked at his door and received no response. He wasn't in his room.

No, he would not have come up to bed without knocking at her door first. Likely, he was still downstairs. Who else was down there with him? She couldn't wander the halls in her nightclothes. But this was no time to be coy. She needed to find him quickly, or she'd never recover the book.

He was just coming up the stairs when she hurried down. He caught her in his arms to stop her from careening into him. "Honey, what's wrong?"

"*The Book of Love* is gone. I think Lady Sarah's taken it." She didn't know why she was so overset, for it was merely a musty, old book. But to her, it was more than that. It was a pathway to love. As she stood on the steps beside Tom, his arms lightly around her shoulders, his eyes gleaming with intelligence, and his gaze comforting and affectionate, she understood what this book had opened her eyes to…the wonder of love.

Yes, she had fallen in love with Tom.

He roused all the right feelings in her, just as the book described. She felt safe. Protected. Secure within his arms.

Oh, she had always been able to take care of herself. Able to run a successful business. But sharing her life with a man? This was so different. This was about opening her heart. Risking her heart.

How could she? To admit she loved him would also mean revealing her secret, so there was no escaping it.

How would he feel then?

It didn't matter. If she wanted him, she had to confide in him. And yes, she wanted him desperately. He was becoming as important to her as the breath of life.

"Honey, you're shaking. Go back to your room and let me take care of this." He caressed her cheek. "She can't hurt me, but she is not above hurting you. I'll make sure she doesn't."

"But—"

"It is my house. My guests. My mistake for inviting them."

She arched an eyebrow. "So, this makes it your problem to fix?"

He nodded. "Lottie is assigned as maid to you and Lady Sarah. I'll let her know to keep an eye out for the book and bring it to me immediately if she finds it. That red leather binding is hard to miss. Lottie's sister, Glenna, was assigned to her two companions for the duration of the party. I'll give her the same instructions and pass the word to all my staff. We'll get it back for you."

"Thank you, Tom. The worst of it is that my sister and cousins trusted me to keep it safe. They believe it has magical powers. Ridiculous, of course. But how can I let them all down by losing it?" Tears welled in her eyes. She did not want him to see her crying, but a stray tear or two fell onto her cheek. "I didn't even want the book. As many times as they handed it to me, I tried to give it back."

"And then you brought it here."

"Only to keep them from bothering me about it. But I was wrong." She sighed and rested her head against his warm, solid chest. "Just reading those first chapters opened my eyes to so much."

"Ah, I think we've made a breakthrough," he teased.

She nodded. "Not quite, but almost."

"Almost?" He kissed the top of her head. "That's a monumental step forward for you, isn't it? We'll explore this further tomorrow, with or without the book. There is wisdom in it, but it isn't a living being, just words on a page. Intelligent, helpful words, but they can never replace what we feel in our hearts."

He eased her out of his arms. "Go to bed, Honey. I'll knock at your door if I've had any success in finding it."

She returned upstairs, and he followed her to see her safely to her room. "Thank you, Tom."

He remained watching as she entered.

She'd left her lamp turned on, not thinking to douse it before running off to find him. She was glad now that she hadn't, for she did not want to be walking into a darkened chamber. But she cried out softly the moment her gaze fell on her night table. "Tom! Tom!" she cried in an urgent whisper. "Look! How is it possible?"

He hurried in.

She pointed to the book, now sitting atop the table. "I don't understand. How did it get back in here?" Picking it up, she began to leaf through the pages. "Upon my oath, it was not here before. I wasn't making it up."

"I believe you."

But he was frowning as his gaze fell on her and then the book. "Someone must have slipped it back in while we were talking on the stairs."

"What if they're still here?" She ran to her wardrobe to make certain no one was hiding in there. Then she peeked under her bed. Lastly, she checked behind the drapes. "This doesn't make any sense."

"I'll ask around tomorrow." He quietly shut the door behind him and stepped into the room. "Now that you have it back, would you like to read more of it this evening?"

She shook her head. "Do you mind if we put it off until tomorrow?"

"No, it's fine." He ran his hand along the back of his neck, obviously wanting to say something more. "Before I go, I want to thank you for what you did today for my mother."

"It was nothing, truly."

He grunted. "You saved the day. It meant everything to me. What was I thinking, having her paint when she hadn't touched a brush in years? And to force her to do it now? All she did was dither and stare at her supplies as though she had never seen them before and didn't know what they were."

"Sit down, Tom." She could see he was getting wound up again, trying to fix something he had no power to fix. For a man used to being in control, the feeling of helplessness had to be agonizing. "I don't have anything to offer you to eat or drink, but we can talk."

He gave a mirthless laugh. "Yes, let's talk. I gave you my oath I wouldn't touch you and I won't. It's a good thing because right now, all I want to do is devour you." He settled in the offered chair and buried his face in his hands for a long moment. "I didn't mean it the way it sounded."

"I know. You're a gentleman."

He grunted again. "No, I'm not really. Even a few months ago, I would have taken up Lady Sarah's invitation and been romping in bed with her and her dim-witted, toady friends. But meeting you changed me. The moment I set eyes on you, it was as though all the pieces of my life suddenly fell into place. I hadn't even spoken to you yet, but I knew you were someone special. And you are. You're the light that shines in dark times."

He dropped his hands to his sides and looked at her. "Whatever this thing is between us needs to run its natural course. But I'll tell you right now, I did not think it possible beauty such as yours could ever exist in the world. And for me to find it? To find you? Well, here you are, and I don't ever want to let you go."

"Tom—"

"No, don't dismiss me. Whatever your terrible secret is, I hope you'll trust me enough to tell me. I still can't imagine how bad it could be. When I look at you, all I see is a woman of extraordinary quality. A woman of infinite kindness and compassion. So many things ran through my mind today. I knew Lady Sarah was going to cause trouble. I know she dislikes you, no doubt because she senses that I like you."

Honey nodded. "Otherwise, she wouldn't pay me any notice. My family is in trade. I'm a nobody to her."

"She's a vindictive brat. I was afraid she would do something to ruin you."

"I worried about it, too." She sank onto the chair beside his and propped her elbows on the table. "She and her two lackeys are probably plotting something dastardly as we speak. I was sure they'd stolen the book. Maybe they were just teasing me with trivial irritations before they sprang their real trap."

"I'd marry you if it came to that." He held up a hand when she opened her mouth to protest. "Before you gasp and declare you wish to remain a spinster, let me tell you my point. Although you must know what I'm about to say since I've already spilled my guts to you."

He took a deep breath. "I'd marry you this very night if I had to. Not because I'd feel honor-bound to do it. I've run away from the parson's trap all my life and am quite adept at escaping it. However, with you, I'd run *toward* it. The thought of sharing a lifetime with you does not make me break out in a sweat or bring on hives."

She couldn't help but grin. "That's quite a romantic statement. You have me swooning."

He arched an eyebrow and smiled back. "Earl baring his soul here. Show a little respect."

She took his hand and held it, entwining her fingers with his. "I'm sorry. Overwhelmed girl here. I never thought anyone as special as you could like me."

"Surely you realize it's more than that. The possibility of waking to the sight of your lovely face each morning, of going about my duties and coming home to your beautiful smile at the end of each day...of building a life and a family with you, is—"

She shot to her feet. "Tom, *no*."

He rose along with her, obviously frustrated. "What am I missing, Honey? Did I misunderstand your willingness last night? Do you not care for me?"

All she had to do was tell him that she didn't like him, and he would stop pursuing her. It would sadden him, perhaps break his heart for a little while. But his heart would mend in time. However, she was beginning to doubt hers ever would. "Give me time, Tom."

"To figure out whether you like me?"

"No. That was never in doubt."

His tension eased. "Then, you like me?"

"Of course, I do."

"Do you love me?"

The air grew charged around them while she struggled to give him an answer.

He caressed her cheek and cast her a wry smile. "If you have to think about it, then the answer to that question is no."

She could feel his heartbreak as though it was living, palpable thing. Brittle. Shattering. Breaking apart like fragile crystal.

She stopped him as he strode to the door. "Ask me again."

His eyes reflected his confusion, perhaps his concern that he would ask again and she would kick him in the teeth with her answer. "Do you love me?"

"Yes, Tom. I do," she said and felt the tension flow out of him.

"Well, that's settled." His smile touched her heart, for it was so warm and tender. "I have more questions for you. Do I dare ask the next one?"

"No. Please, not tonight." She knew what it would be.

He wanted to know her secret.

"Honey—"

"No. But if you'd like to know when I fell in love with you, that I will answer. I think it was at first sight. How deeply do I love you? Very. So deeply, it hurts."

Those answers were easy.

But this conversation was between an earl and the girl he thought was of respectable birth.

How different would it be if he knew she was illegitimate?

CHAPTER EIGHT

T OM STIFLED HIS disappointment.

Honey was not among the small party gathered in the entry hall shortly after daybreak, preparing to go down to the river to fish. Two footmen stood beside the lords and ladies, fishing poles and other supplies in their hands.

"Shall we go, Wycke?" Lord Wrexham asked, peering at him through bloodshot eyes.

Tom was surprised his friend had made it down this early, especially since he suspected Wrexham had been cavorting with Lady Sarah in her bedchamber last night. "Yes, let's. My butler will point any stragglers in the right direction. We won't be hard to find."

Perhaps it was for the best Honey wasn't here to distract him. As it was, he could not get her off his mind. After their talk, he'd returned to his bedchamber, stripped out of his clothes, and fallen into bed alone.

Aching and alone, for he hadn't taken another woman to his bed since setting eyes on the girl.

What was it about her?

She'd done little more than smile at him. So how could she so thoroughly possess his heart upon a mere two days of closer acquaintance?

Indeed, he hardly knew her.

They'd never spoken at length before this weekend. He'd first met her about three months ago at one of those London teas. Since then, he'd mostly watched her from a distance. If they spoke, it was in passing, an occasional greeting that never lasted more than a minute or two.

And yet, last night, he was ready to propose to her.

No wonder she'd stopped him; he was moving too fast.

He'd given his sister and Malcolm no end of grief when they'd wanted to marry quickly. And here he was, ready to make Honey his countess after a mere two days.

She still had this secret she feared to tell him.

A light mist swirled around his boots as he led the others to the river. He knew the path well, for he often came out here on his own to think and fish. It did not matter the season, this was his spot when seeking solace.

Ten guests had braved the early hour to join him, seven men and three young ladies. No one spoke. It was too early, and most of the men were still hungover from last night.

Leaves crunched beneath their feet as they marched along the path that meandered through the meadow and along the arches of trees. Soon, he heard the gentle *whoosh* of flowing water and the chirp of birds amid the shrubs along the riverbank. "This is the spot. Grab your fishing poles and spread out along the shore. Does anyone require assistance?"

All three young ladies replied in the affirmative, batting their eyelashes and smiling at him. Yes, of course. He'd walked straight into that one.

He helped each of them, enduring more batted eyelashes and feigned smiles. Well, perhaps he was being harsh. They were under pressure from their families to marry and had little time to accomplish the feat. There were four other bachelors among their party. He assigned three of them the task of attending to the ladies.

The fourth one was so deeply hungover, Tom was afraid the man would tumble into the water. He took a spot near him, ready to haul him out of the river if he actually did fall in. But he'd done his service to the ladies. He grinned as they seemed to happily pair off with their assigned partners.

A few other guests strolled down to join them an hour later, Honey among them. She'd walked down with Pip and Periwinkle. "Care to take a turn, Pip?" he asked as they approached.

The boy was unable to contain his excitement. "Yes, may I?"

Tom handed over his pole and gave him a few tips on how to dab it in the water to attract the fish. He then turned to Honey. "I could send one of the footmen back for more fishing poles. Or would you rather take a walk along the bank with me?"

"A walk would be lovely, my lord."

They stayed within sight of their group, but far enough away so as not to be overheard. Honey spoke first. "You left early to go fishing, and I thought you might not have had time to speak to Lottie or her sister. So, I mentioned the odd disappearance of my book to Lottie when she came up to help me dress. She said you'd already advised all of them. Thank you, Tom."

He nodded.

"She assured me she'd keep an ear to the ground and would check with everyone on your staff throughout the day. But it's still so odd. It has me puzzled. I suppose I ought to stop thinking about it. After all, it is a crime that never happened."

"It did happen," he corrected. "Perhaps one of Sarah's toadies took it, then realized she might get herself into serious trouble and quickly put it back."

Honey nodded. "Yes, it could be. Or even Poppy borrowing it, but she would have mentioned something about it to me this morning while we ate our breakfast. When I told her what happened, she grew concerned and told me to hide it away."

"Did you?"

She nodded. "I gave it to your valet and told him you had asked for it. I told him to put it in your quarters right away and make certain no one touches it. Lady Sarah and her rabble might not hesitate to enter my bedchamber, but they would never dare enter yours."

Tom shook his head and groaned. "You gave Merrick that book? *The Book of Love? Bollocks*. I'll never hear the end of it from that damn Scot. He'll tease me about it 'til the day he takes his last breath."

Honey's eyes rounded in dismay. "Oh, dear. I didn't mean... I'll tell him I made a mistake, and you weren't asking for the book."

"I'm jesting. Merrick and I will have a good chuckle over it, that's all. I wouldn't be surprised if I caught him reading it. He's a cantankerous old goat on the outside, but soft as pudding on the inside."

She looked at him with her eyes gleaming. "And you, Tom? What are you?"

He shrugged. "I never gave it much thought until you came along. What sort of person do you think I am?"

"That's an easy one. You already know how I feel about you. Obviously, I believe you're the best sort of man."

"But you don't trust me."

"Ah, we're back to that. You want to know my secret." She nibbled her lip, and the smile glowing in her eyes now faded. "I do trust you. But it is not something I can lightly talk about. Let's get through your weekend party first."

She was right.

How could he expect her to confide in him? Whatever her secret, he could not believe she had done anything wrong to precipitate it.

She was honest, that much was obvious. Despite their interlude the other night, a kiss that had been taken too far, she was of the highest moral character. Who else would have confessed to having a damaging secret before marriage?

Any other debutante would have kept silent until he had married her, and it was too late for him to annul their marriage.

Not Honey.

She did not have it in her to deceive him.

"You look lovely, by the way." He ought to have mentioned it sooner. But she always looked beautiful, never more so than when she wore these unadorned day gowns. This one was a pale blue that somehow brought out the shimmering blue of her eyes.

"Thank you. You're looking quite handsome yourself. But you always do." She cast him an impish grin. "I'm sure you have no idea how quickly you set every girl's heart aflutter. As you know, I am no exception. Mad flutters, the moment I saw you standing by the river."

"You affect me, too. As you well know from the other night." But he said no more as he heard Periwinkle suddenly frantically *yip*. The muddy ground beneath the dog's feet began to give away.

Honey gasped. "Oh, no! Tom, he's falling into the river."

"Bollocks! Pip just jumped in after him. Can the boy swim?" He tossed off his jacket and ran toward the water.

Honey tried her best to keep up with him. "I don't know."

Tom dove in. Whether or not the boy could swim no longer mattered. The river current was too strong for the lad to handle while also holding on to Periwinkle. He reached them in two strokes, grabbed Pip just as the boy lost his grip on Lavinia's dog, and shoved him to shore. Honey and two of the men were there to help pull him out of the water.

Tom then swam to Periwinkle, overtaking him as he frantically tried to paddle his way to shore. But he was a little dog, and the current was too swift for him to handle. He grabbed the frightened pup in one arm. But knowing he couldn't fight the current swimming with only one arm, he floated along with it until he finally caught a protruding branch and used it to swing himself closer to shore.

Honey and a few more of the men in their fishing party had been running parallel to him all the while. Honey was first to him, grabbing Periwinkle while the men helped to haul him out of the water and onto the grass.

He laughed and coughed and took several deep breaths.

"Lord Wycke, are you all right?" Honey knelt beside him, her face ashen.

Lavinia's waterlogged spaniel was shivering and squirming in her arms. Pip was still dripping water from every pore as he ran up to him and dropped to his knees beside him.

"Thank you," the boy said and hugged him.

He wrapped his arms around the frightened boy. "Are you all right, Pip?"

He nodded. "Yes, thanks to you."

Everyone then began to ask if he was all right.

"Yes, all of you. I'm fine." He was still breathing heavily and coughing. His clothes and boots were soaked. But otherwise, he'd suffered no damage.

Honey remained beside him as the other men helped Pip and Periwinkle back to the house. "Tom, you were brilliant."

"Brilliant enough for a kiss?" He took her hand.

"Not here!" But she nodded. "Yes, later. As many as you wish." She slipped her hand out of his and scrambled to her feet just as the rest of their party approached.

Everyone fussed over him the entire way back to the house, but he kept his eyes on Honey, who was walking with the other young ladies. He was glad to see they were keeping her company, for he didn't want her to be ignored in all the commotion.

He glanced back toward the river and saw that his footmen were collecting the fishing poles and baskets of food that had been brought down with them. The guests at the house ran out to him, all chattering at once, congratulating him and asking him to tell them every detail of what had happened.

He had no idea what Pip had just told them, but he was now surrounded by an eager throng who treated him as though he was Julius

Caesar returned from conquering empires. He couldn't take a step without someone cheering or patting him on the back.

He answered a few questions but left it to the others in his party to relate the tale while he went upstairs to change out of his wet clothes. Nathaniel and Poppy had taken Pip upstairs. Lavinia was still downstairs, crying as his staff fussed over Periwinkle. They were drying him with towels and offering him all manner of treats.

He looked around for Honey, but he'd been delayed by everyone lauding him as a returning hero. She must have gone up ahead of him because he lost sight of her.

His valet was waiting for him as he squished down the hall and entered his bedchamber. "Don't you dare laugh at me, Merrick, or I shall sack your fat, Scottish arse."

"Very well, my lord. As you wish." But he was grinning like one of those barnyard cats who'd just caught a bird in his mouth. "A job well done, my lord."

"Anyone could have done it." He stripped out of his shirt, pants, and boots.

"But only you dove in."

Tom chuckled. "Is that a smile of admiration I detect?"

"A smile? On me? Heaven forbid. Would you care for a towel?" He held one out to him.

Tom took it and quickly dried himself off. "Miss Farthingale brought me a book," he said, reaching for the dry trousers and boots. "Where did you put it?"

The man was still tossing him that irritating grin. "In your bureau. Top drawer. She's the best of the lot," he said, offering an opinion he wasn't asked. "It's about time you got around to business."

Tom was going to toss back a remark when someone pounded on his door. "Lord Wycke! Lord Wycke!"

It was Honey.

He'd already donned fresh pants and boots, so he quickly tossed on his shirt and opened the door. She still wore the gown soiled during Periwinkle's rescue. One look at her expression, and he knew something was terribly wrong. "What's happened?"

"Your mother is missing."

"Bloody hell. Where's Dora? When did she notice her gone?" He turned away to hastily tuck in his shirt and then strode toward his mother's chamber. Honey doubled her steps to keep up with his strides.

"She can't have been gone long. Dora said she only left her for a few minutes."

He raked a hand through his wet hair. "Damn it. She shouldn't have left her at all."

"You mustn't blame her." Honey rolled her eyes. "The poor woman has to occasionally take care of her own necessities. I'll help you search. I sent Lottie downstairs to alert the staff. I'm sorry, I should have asked you first. But you were still surrounded by everyone. All I could think of was to get them out searching before she came to any harm."

He nodded. "It's all right, Honey. You did what you had to do."

Dora was sitting in his mother's quarters with her hands clasped in her lap. She was crying, so whatever admonishment Tom had thought to give no longer seemed important. It was his fault for placing the entire burden on her. This behavior was new to all of them. "We'll find her, Dora," he said, patting her hands. "Do you have any idea where she might have gone?"

She glanced over his shoulder to gaze at Honey. "Miss Farthingale asked me the same question, but I don't know. We were speaking of you and Lady Anne, and how much you all enjoyed your summers here. Before that, we spoke of our tea and scones, and discussed what gown she would wear to supper this evening."

"My lord," Honey said, "was there a favorite place you used to go as children? Perhaps a favorite activity?"

"Not that I can think of. We used to go walking with my father. My mother was always busy doing something in the house or painting on the veranda."

"Not always on the veranda. Some of her paintings were scenes of the garden or of the river." Her eyes widened in alarm.

"Bloody hell! She can't have gone to the river." But he grabbed Honey's hand and took off with her down the servants' stairs, hoping not to be seen by the other guests. "We've just come from there. I wonder if she heard everyone's comments when we returned with Pip and Periwinkle, and it put the river in her mind."

They had almost reached this morning's fishing spot when he realized he was still holding Honey's hand. It felt so right and natural, as though she was his lifeline. Indeed, he needed to hold on to her for fear of drowning, for he was woefully unprepared to handle his mother's deteriorating health.

He released her hand, and they split up, Honey searching upstream, and he taking the trail downstream.

He encountered several footmen who had just begun searching along the river. "We looked for Lady Wycke in the barn, the stables, the garden, and down the long drive to the front gate. No sign of her in any of those places, m'lord."

"Thank you. It helps to rule those out." He knew Mrs. Finch and the maids were searching the house, quietly going room to room on the chance she'd wandered into one of the guest quarters. "Miss Farthingale is searching the north trail. Simon, catch up to her and help her out. John and Peter, come with me."

Upstream was less treacherous. He hoped his mother had gone in that direction, assuming she had strayed to the river. They'd catch up to her if she were walking the trail. She couldn't have gone far. But if she'd fallen in?

He shook his head. *No.* She was afraid of water. She wasn't a swimmer.

He sent John and Peter on ahead, having them run to the edge of his property. He proceeded slower, keeping his eye on the water to his right and the woods to his left. He heard footsteps pounding behind him and heard Simon call to him. "My lord, Miss Farthingale has found her!"

"Thank the Graces. Let John and Peter know. How is she? Able to walk back to the house on her own?"

"I think so, m'lord. Miss Farthingale was holding her hand and trying to calm her down. But your mum was asking for you. 'Where's Tom? Where's my Tom?' she kept saying."

"I'll go to her at once. Thank you all for your assistance." He retraced his steps and kept running along the trail until he encountered Honey seated on the trunk of a fallen tree, her arm around his mother.

She glanced up at him with open relief.

His mother noticed him as well. "Tom, where have you been? I've been waiting for you. You've been gone so long."

"I'm right here, my darling. Shall we walk back to the house now?" He held out his arm to her. She took it as though nothing was amiss, unaware she had just sent the household into utter panic.

They entered the house by way of the kitchen and made their way up the servants' stairs. Tom was drained, his feelings raw by the time they finally settled her in her quarters. When Dora took over the care of his mother, Honey returned to her room to finally change out of her gown. He stayed a little while longer to make certain his mother had calmed.

"Tom, I'm quite tired from our walk. Would you mind if I had my supper in our room tonight?"

Our room?

She thought he was his father.

"Not at all, my darling." He kissed her brow and left to go in search of Mrs. Finch. He found his able housekeeper talking to his staff about the evening's entertainments. He interrupted her briefly to ask for a maid to assist Dora for the remainder of their stay.

"Yes, my lord. I shall see to it at once."

He returned to his quarters to wash and change again. "Miss Far-thingale found her, Merrick."

His valet nodded. "We are all worried about your dear mother. Miss Farthingale seems to have a gentle way with her."

He snorted. "I need a brandy."

"I'll bring up the entire bottle. You look as though a mere glass won't do."

He groaned and ran a hand through his hair. It was still wet from his earlier plunge into the river to save Pip and Periwinkle. "I can't wait until this party is over and everyone leaves. It isn't even midday, and I already feel spent. I dread what this afternoon will bring. The next time I suggest a house party, just kick me."

Merrick smiled. "With pleasure, my lord."

To his surprise, the afternoon passed quietly. The sky grew over-cast, and rain began to fall in torrents shortly after luncheon, so card tables were set up in the music room while teapots and trays of pies and cakes were set up in the drawing room. Those who did not wish to indulge in either could play billiards or quietly read in his library, where he suspected he'd find Honey since she wasn't anywhere else in the house.

Her book about love was still safely tucked away in his bedcham-ber. He wasn't certain when they'd have the chance to read it together. Perhaps this evening, once everyone had retired to bed. It was dangerous business sneaking into her chamber or having her sneak into his, but he truly did not care if they were caught. After today, he could not imagine sharing his life with anyone but her.

He strolled into the library and saw her seated on the sofa with one of his books in hand. He was curious as to which one. She was a romantic but also had a good business head. Which side would win out?

They were not alone, so he kept his conversation to casual comments about the weather and the book she'd chosen to read. It was a book on herbs and spices. "For our soaps and lotions," she explained. "Belle is really the expert, but I also like to learn as much as I can since these often go into our products, and I ought to know what I sell. Their medicinal properties are also very interesting."

The levelheaded business side won out.

But the smile she cast him was soft and gentle, very much that of a young woman hopeful of love. Had they been alone, he would have had her in his arms, the book tossed aside, and he would have been kissing her with all his heart and soul.

"What are you going to read?" she asked.

"No book, just the newspaper." He'd ordered several delivered each day so that his guests did not have to fight over who would read them first. He picked up one of the copies and settled in the chair beside hers. "By the way, was my staff able to take the stains out of the gown you wore this morning?"

She grimaced. "They're working on it. I'm not sure."

"Well, add it to yesterday's gown. I'll owe you a new wardrobe by the time this party is over."

She shook her head and laughed. "As long as I'm left with one to wear home. I'd hate to have to travel in clothes borrowed from you."

"They'd be a little big on you." Although he found the notion appealing, the thought of her sleeping in one of his shirts, her vanilla scent clinging to the fabric... He cleared his throat and returned his attention to the newspaper.

After a few minutes, the library door opened, and Lady Sarah and her two toadies strolled in. *Bollocks.* Had she not tired of causing trouble? He knew these ladies hadn't come in here to read, for there wasn't a decent brain among them.

He watched them from behind his newspaper.

They were eying Honey.

He swore silently and rose. "Miss Farthingale, I believe they've set out the desserts. Will you join me in the drawing room?"

"That sounds delightful." She set aside her book and took his offered arm. "Thank you for getting me out of there. What is wrong with those girls? Can they do nothing but plot mischief?" she grumbled as they walked to the drawing room.

"It seems not. Excuse me, Honey. I don't trust them alone in my library. I have some valuable artifacts in there."

He returned in time to see them struggling to break the glass on one of the medieval manuscripts.

"Sarah! He's back!" One of her peahen friends cried out.

He grabbed Sarah, then glowered at her friends, wordlessly warning them to follow him out. The look he cast must have terrified the pair because they burst into tears. He didn't care. He'd had enough of their antics. He ordered them into his study, then left to fetch Lady Sarah's father. "Your Grace," he said, interrupting the Duke of Remson's card game. "Forgive me, but I require a moment of your time."

The man must have suspected what was coming. He rose without fuss and excused himself from the hand. "What has she done now, Wycke?"

"I caught her and her friends in the library, trying to break the glass on the Corinthian manuscript. Take her home, Your Grace. Make up any excuse you like. But this is beyond nursery room antics. I cannot allow her or her friends to remain."

It would be a simple matter since the duke had brought the two girls along with his daughter, so he could take them all away without fuss. They entered the study and closed the door behind them. Sarah's two friends were still weeping, now uncontrollably. Sarah was standing beside his desk, her expression as cold as ice.

"Daughter, what do you have to say for yourself?"

She didn't blink as her father approached. "I was bored."

"Bored? Is this all you have to offer? What is wrong with you? You've been given every opportunity in life, never had to worry about your next meal or a roof over your head. You've had the finest instructors, every advantage, and you set about destroying your host's valuable property because you're bored? Perhaps a month in a Cheapside workhouse will keep you occupied. What do you say to that?"

"You wouldn't dare. It would make you a laughingstock."

The duke looked as though he wanted to hit her. In truth, she deserved a good spanking, but the man was enraged, and Tom was concerned he might do her serious harm. He stepped between them. "Take her home, Your Grace. She's showing off in front of her friends."

He turned to the weeping girls, hoping their tears meant they understood wrong from right. "Lady Sarah does not seem to have learned anything from this. I hope you both have better sense. Why do you think none of the bachelors will come near you? They are not blind to your idiocy or to your friend's poison. If you ever hope to marry, keep your distance from her. She'll ruin your lives along with her own."

Lady Amelia dabbed her handkerchief to her nose. "I'm sorry, Lord Wycke. We wouldn't have harmed it. We were just curious to look at that ancient book."

Lady Jenna nodded. "We would have been careful."

"You would have destroyed it. The pages are too fragile. But Lady Sarah knows this." He sighed and shook his head. "You two need to start thinking for yourselves. Or develop a better sense of whom to trust. Go upstairs and pack your things. I'll send up maids to help you. You're all leaving here first thing in the morning."

They looked quite miserable about it. He only hoped they'd taken his words to heart, but he had little faith they had. The two were already looking at Sarah as though silently pleading to tell them what to do.

Heaven help them.

He started to walk out to give the duke a moment of privacy with the young ladies but stopped first to address Sarah. "If you take a toe out of line from now till then, I shall toss you out this very night." He turned to her father. "I'm sorry, Your Grace. This is not something I do lightly. Your family and mine have been friends for decades. But there is an unhealthy rage built up inside your daughter. She needs help, not visits to her modiste or more dance instruction."

He shut the door quietly behind him as he strode out.

He couldn't wait until those three were gone.

His concern was not for himself, but for Honey. Because of him, she had become the target of Lady Sarah's rage. He was going to keep a close eye on her tonight.

He hoped he was wrong about the duke's daughter.

But he trusted his instincts, and those instincts were warning him Sarah meant to cause trouble.

But how? And when?

CHAPTER NINE

TOM KNEW HE should have waited until the following morning to see Honey, but she was a fire in his blood, and he could not pass the night without having her in his presence. She calmed him. She soothed him. Were it not for her, he'd likely be behaving as badly as the Duke of Remson's daughter. Perhaps not as outwardly destructive. He was never one to hurt others. No, he'd turn that wrath inward, only hurting himself.

For this reason, he hoped the duke could do something to help his daughter. But right now, there was no telling what this girl would do. Her rage was not something he'd ever seen in her when she was younger. He suspected it had something to do with her mother's passing. The two had been very close.

But he could offer no advice on how to fix her pain. He couldn't handle his own mother's failing health. He put all of it out of his mind as he knocked lightly on Honey's door. Everyone else had gone to bed…or off to whatever assignations arranged earlier.

A storm raged outside, the wind blowing and rain pounding with enough force to rattle the windows and take down some trees. The weather matched his turbulent mood. Thunderous. Howling. "It's me," he whispered through the door. "Let me in."

He carried the book with him but wasn't certain they'd get through any of it this night.

She opened the door, but instead of stepping aside to allow him in, she came into the hall and shut the door behind them. "We're going to read in the library."

This explained why she had yet to change out of her gown or let down her hair, that beautiful mass of burnished copper-gold curls. He ached to bury his hands in those silken curls. "Don't you trust me?" he asked in jest, for not even he trusted himself just now.

She cast him a soft look along with a wistful smile. "You gave me your oath. I know you wouldn't break it. I trust you. It's me I don't trust. I'd release you from your promise if we remained alone in my bedchamber. So, we're going to the library where it's safe."

Safe?

How little this girl knew about men.

He didn't need a bed to take her. When thinking with his low, lusting brain—which meant he wasn't thinking at all—he could take her anywhere. On a table. Against the shelves. On his desk. On the carpet. "I'll go in first to make certain no one's in there."

"Why? We're only reading a book."

He took her hand to guide her down the stairs in darkness. "You and I alone, in the middle of the night. No one would believe us even if they found us doing nothing but reading."

"I suppose you're right. We could wait until tomorrow. Daylight."

He gave a laughing groan. "We could, and we should, but I can't. You're important to me, Honey. For both our sakes, I need to understand what I'm feeling. I need to get this right."

"You could have read the book on your own."

"No, we have to do this together. At least, I believe so. Maybe it isn't the same for everyone else. I don't know. As for me, I can't do this without you." He peered into the library and saw that it was empty.

He took her hand to guide her in and kept hold of it even after he'd shut the door behind them. It was pitch dark, and he didn't want her bumping into a table or chair. He could walk through this house with his eyes closed and not bump into anything, he knew it so well.

He released her hand a moment to light a lamp, then carried it and the book to a small table by the sofa. He set the lamp down on the table. "Have a seat, Honey. Let's get started."

He settled beside her, putting his arm around her to draw her closer. She nestled against his chest. Neither of them immediately realized what they'd done, falling into this position as though it was the most natural thing in the world. When Honey noticed, she tried to scamper away, but he held her back. "The point of this book is to understand our feelings and learn to trust what feels right."

She rested her head against his chest. "Everything feels right with you."

"That's a good thing." He chuckled.

"No." She sighed. "I thought it would be safer for us in here, but I don't think I'm safe with you anywhere."

"You're safe with me *everywhere*. I'd never do anything to hurt you."

"Tom, it isn't you I'm worried about. It's me. Falling in love with you has made matters worse for me, not better. I came to your house party thinking I could get an unforgettable kiss from England's handsomest bachelor. Just a kiss. That's all I thought would satisfy me. Then I'd go on my merry spinster way and relive your kiss every night in my dreams."

"It doesn't have to be a dream."

"For now, it does. You don't know my secret yet, and I'm still not certain how you will take it when I tell you. And before you get angry," she said, feeling the sudden tension in his body, "were you not an earl from one of the oldest and most respected families in the realm, perhaps I would not be as concerned. I don't know how this will turn out with a man like you. But you're right. Let's read through the book. Whatever is meant to happen will happen."

That damn secret.

"Very well. Where did we leave off? The sense of touch. Well, I think we have that one well in hand. No pun intended. What do you feel when I touch you, Honey?"

"I suppose you want the truth."

He arched an eyebrow and grinned. "It would be helpful."

"I feel happiness beyond anything I've ever felt before. It's a little frightening actually. There's so much a touch can convey. When you took my hand as we made our way in here, it was as though you were speaking to me. *You're safe with me. I will protect you.* This is what your touch told me. Even the other night when you naughtily untied the ribbon of my nightgown, I knew what we were doing was dangerous. But I didn't want you to stop. I wasn't scared. In my heart, I knew you'd never hurt me."

She raised her head to look up at him. "What do you feel when you touch me?"

His arm tightened around her. "Something beyond my low brain urge to mate. That urge is always lurking beneath the surface, of course. You know, burning desire. Fiery torment. You touch me, and I burst into flames."

She grinned up at him. "You hide it very well. Seriously, I couldn't tell."

"That's because I try not to show it when we're among others. I try not to show it when alone with you, because you've always been more than a mere lusting game for me."

She arched her eyebrow in that impudent way he thought charming. Honey had a compassionate soul, but she also had that tinge of fire to her hair and an impish bit of the devil in her that made her always interesting. "What are you saying? That you'd never abandon me to be eaten by wolves?"

"Never. If you feel safe and protected, it is because you are. That urge to guard you, to watch over you like a protective wolf, is ingrained in my heart. I've told you from the start, you aren't a dalliance for me. I knew it at first glance."

He kissed the top of her head. "What confuses me is how I would know this before we'd ever exchanged words. I suppose this is the importance of not rushing into anything. What seems perfect might not be. This is what I feared for Anne when she and Malcolm rushed into their commitment. But these past few days have shown me that my gut instinct was right about you. So, moving beyond my lower brain desires, when I'm with you, I feel as though you are that missing part of me. A part that makes me a better person than I am on my own. I know whatever problems I face will be conquered because I have you by my side. How's that for honesty?"

"Quite perfect. This book wreaks havoc on one's emotions, doesn't it?"

"It merely draws them out, makes you face what you are feeling without blinders on. I think it shows you how all these senses are connected. Taste, touch, sight, and so on. They enhance one's understanding of love, but only if we're ready to accept the truth."

"And when we're not, the example is in Wellington's love gone wrong?"

He nodded. "The same could be said of Lord Wrexham fawning over Lady Sarah. He's playing with fire and will be badly scorched if he doesn't open his eyes to her faults."

"Maybe he's pretending and is only after her father's wealth. You did say there were several fortune hunters among the party."

"Wrexham isn't in dire straits. Perhaps he likes to live dangerously. As for me, I prefer to keep the chaos out of my home."

She laughed. "Then the last thing you want is to attach yourself to a Farthingale. We travel in massive herds, like beasts migrating along the Serengeti plains. Except we migrate to London from all over England. Oxfordshire, Yorkshire, Devonshire."

He chuckled.

"I don't know how Uncle John and Aunt Sophie haven't gone

insane hosting all of us throughout the years. We attract trouble. You saw what happened to Finn. He was in Lady Dayne's garden, minding his own business one moment, and in the next, he was struck down by my sister. Same for his cousin, Romulus. He simply walked by to check on his new house, heard a scream, and ran into a wall of bees and Violet."

"They've adapted quite well to marriage."

She laughed. "Fortunately. My point is, forget about peace and quiet. It does not exist in a Farthingale household. Plus, we meddle in everyone's business."

"There's a difference. Your family chaos arises out of love. That's an important distinction." He closed the book when he noticed Honey stifling a yawn. "I see that I am boring you," he teased. "It's late. Let me take you upstairs. To your quarters. I won't go in. We know it's too dangerous to be anywhere near you in a room with a bed."

She nodded. "I am tired. It has been a long day."

"We'll read more about the wonder of love tomorrow." He'd scanned a few pages ahead and knew the next chapters dug beyond the five senses, discussing how shared connections and expectations kept love strong and ever-building.

Surprisingly, he seemed to be more intrigued by this book than Honey was. Perhaps it was because of his experience with women. He'd come across so many and had so many thrust at him that to suddenly meet the one who felt so right when all others had felt so wrong…it was something precious that he needed to pursue.

He did not want to make a misstep and destroy what could be the best thing ever to happen to him.

He took her hand, once more amazed by how soft and right it felt in his. He held a candle in his other hand as they quietly climbed the stairs together. He saw himself doing just this, night after night, as they retired to bed as husband and wife.

Not a single pang of fear shot through him.

It was surprising how little he dreaded a lifetime commitment with this girl. How could he let Honey go once the party was over? She was making him wait to learn her secret, but it seemed to him, waiting would only make matters worse. If her fears came to pass and it was something that prevented him from marrying her, then prolonging the silence would break both their hearts.

Him? Heartbroken? After an acquaintance of only two days?

Was it possible for love to take root so deeply in that short a time?

"Oh, no!" Honey's whispered cry shook him out of his thoughts. They'd reached her door and it was open. He knew they'd shut it before going downstairs.

What new mischief was this?

He handed her the book and nudged her behind him. "Let me go in first. Stay out here until I know it's safe."

Bollocks.

He held up the candle and stepped inside. His eyes had adjusted sufficiently to the dim glow of candlelight that he would notice any moving shadows. But there were none. He crossed to her bureau and set the candle atop it, then began to look around. "Lord Almighty."

The wardrobe doors were flung open, and someone had taken a scissor to two of Honey's gowns. His first thought was relief Honey had been in the library with him and not in here. Otherwise, the intruder might have taken the scissors to her.

He shuddered.

This sweet, precious girl might have been cut to ribbons, just as the perpetrator had done with these gowns.

"Tom, what's wrong?" Honey came up behind him, realized what had happened, and flew into his outstretched arms. "Why would anyone do such a thing?"

He cupped her face as she began to tremble. "I don't know."

"Do you think it was Lady Sarah? Is it possible she's that cruel?"

"Until this moment, I didn't think so. But how well can we know what lies in anyone's heart when seeing them only occasionally over the years? She is the likely suspect, isn't she? I've had one of my staff keep an eye on her. Simon will know if she's left her chamber."

"She might have slipped out through the servants' staircase."

"No, there's no secret panel or staircase in her room. She would have had to walk out into the hallway."

He held her in his arms a moment longer before releasing her to draw her a chair. "Let me talk to him. He's just down the hall. Just give me a minute. Don't leave here. I'll be right back."

Simon was one of his most capable and trusted footmen. There was no question he would remain awake and alert while standing guard at the other end of the hallway. But Tom's mind was reeling. Petty behavior was one thing, and Sarah was certainly capable of that. But to destroy someone's clothing? To him, that spoke of rot within one's heart.

The man was surprised to see him. "M'lord? Is something wrong?"

Tom nodded. "Yes, Simon. Very. Has Lady Sarah left her quarters this evening?"

"No. Nor have her two friends."

"Are you certain?"

"Aye, m'lord."

Tom raked a hand through his hair. "Have you seen anyone walk out from a bedchamber at this end of the hall? Or heard noises from anyone's room?"

"No one walked out, although several gents were popping into the rooms of some of your lady guests. They didn't see me. I stayed in the shadows. As for noise..." Simon blushed. "None other than the sort one would expect when a gent goes into a lady's room in the dead of night."

"Damn. Thank you, Simon. Keep a close watch. Someone broke into Miss Farthingale's room and slashed her gowns. This is serious. She might have been injured."

His eyes widened. "I'll keep alert, so you needn't worry. I'll notify your lordship if I see or hear anything more."

Tom strode back to Honey's room, trying to piece it all together. If no one had come down from the other end of the hall, then that only left the few rooms near his end. Nathaniel and Poppy's. Lavinia's. Pip's. His mother's quarters. Honey's guestroom. But Honey had been with him all the while, and her gowns had been fine then.

When he returned to her a short while later, he saw that her eyes were still wide with fright, and her face was ashen. He took her into his arms again. "We'll find the culprit, I promise you. Hush, Honey," he said when he saw a lone tear stream down her cheek. "I'll wake Mrs. Finch. She'll have Lottie clean up the damage and stay with you tonight."

She nodded.

He wished he could stay with her, but there would be no escaping her ruin if he were found here in the morning. It wouldn't matter the reason or the crime. Besides, he had investigating to do.

She cast him a mirthless smile. "What do we now? Who else could it have been but Lady Sarah?"

"She is the likely suspect, but Simon saw no one leave or enter her bedchamber. I doubt she climbed out through her window in the midst of a storm and somehow managed to break in downstairs then steal into your room. Nor could she have climbed from the outside up into here. Your window hasn't been touched, and there's no rain spatter inside."

"But if not her or her friends, who else would it be?"

"No one in their right mind, that's for sure."

He'd tugged the bellpull to summon Mrs. Finch, but expected she'd take a few moments to dress and run up here. As they waited in silence, he heard a commotion in his mother's bedchamber next door. By Honey's expression, he knew she was thinking the same thing he was—that someone had now broken into his mother's quarters, too.

"Stay here."

"I'm coming with you. Your mother and Dora are in their night-clothes. You can't just burst in. But I can." She darted in front of him before he could stop her and ran next door.

She put her ear to the door for just a moment and then hurried in. Tom was right behind her. But the sight stopped them both in their tracks. "Oh, bollocks. Bloody, bloody, bollocks."

Pain tore through him. "Honey, I'm sorry," he said in a ragged whisper.

She took his hand. "It isn't your fault."

Of course it was. It had to be. His mother was sitting with scissors on her lap. Scraps of Honey's two gowns had been ripped apart and were strewn across her bed. She was quietly humming to herself as she moved them around, turning them this way and that. A sewing basket was at the foot of her bed. She seemed to be making a patchwork quilt or something of the sort.

Dora had fallen asleep in a chair while the maid he'd assigned to watch his mother was stretched out in front of the fireplace hearth, curled up in a blanket.

Rage built up inside of him.

Honey would not release his hand. "Isn't it obvious what happened?" she said in a whisper. "Dora and your maid are taking turns sitting up through the night. It was Dora's turn, and she fell asleep. I think you need two maids on rotation in the evening. Dora is getting too feeble. And you can't expect the poor maid," she said, motioning to the sleeping girl, "to work all day and stay up all night."

"Damn it, Honey," he said, his voice low and gravelly. "They should have been watching her."

"I know. But right now, I'm more relieved that we don't have a deranged duke's daughter on our hands. Poor Lady Sarah. Now I wonder if she had anything to do with *The Book of Love* going missing. I hate to think we might have falsely accused her."

She went to his mother's side and sat on the bed next to her. "What a pretty thing you're making, Lady Wycke."

His mother smiled and set aside the scissors while she showed Honey the pretty patches. Honey smoothly took the scissors and handed them to him. They were big, sharp. Able to do harm if used as a weapon. Not that his mother would ever knowingly harm anyone. But she was in her state of unknowing right now.

She might be capable of anything.

Would she remember any of this come morning?

"See the pretty colors?" she asked Honey.

"Yes, they are quite beautiful. But it's late, Lady Wycke. Are you not tired? What if I put these pretty patches in your sewing basket, and you can show them to Dora tomorrow morning? You ought to rest now."

His mother allowed her to set the squares of her torn gowns in the basket. "I can't sleep yet. I'm waiting for my Tom. He must be looking upon the children. He dotes on them, you know."

Honey glanced at him. "Yes, they are lovely children. I'm sure they love you both very much."

His mother frowned and began to look around worriedly. "Where's my Tom?"

Tom inhaled sharply and then let out his breath in a groan of despair. She was thinking of his father again. The rage washed out of him. He swallowed hard, uncertain he was able to speak for the ache that tore through him. Finally, he stepped forward. "I'm right here, my darling. Go to sleep now. You must be very tired."

"Oh, Tom. There you are. Where have you been?" She didn't await his answer, not that he was capable of saying anything more at the moment, and curled up in her bed. Within a matter of minutes, she'd fallen sound asleep.

Honey gently woke the sleeping maid and showed her that Dora was not watching his mother. The maid was horrified. "Miss Farthingale, I didn't realize. She assured me we could switch on and off."

"I know. Dora isn't up to the task. I think Lord Wycke will need to add staff to attend to both of them."

The maid blanched when she realized he was also in the room. He sighed. "It's all right, Glenna. But as Miss Farthingale said, this duty is more than just one person can handle. I'll have Mrs. Finch send up someone to assist you. While you both were sleeping, my mother left her room and damaged two of Miss Farthingale's gowns. You'll find scraps of them in her sewing basket. Someone must always remain awake in here. She cannot go wandering about the house when she slips into her...condition."

They waited for Mrs. Finch to join them, told her the problem, and then it was decided to leave all as it was until the morning. Honey refused the need for a maid in her room. "Lottie will take care of the damage in the morning. We're sorry we troubled you, Mrs. Finch."

"Not at all, Miss Farthingale. You must have been quite alarmed." She sighed and shook her head. "I'll put my best girls on rotation in here going forward."

Once everyone had left his mother's quarters, and only he and Honey remained in the hall, she took his hand and quietly led him into her room. He sank into a chair and buried his face in his hands. This was getting to be an unpleasant routine. "I don't know what to say other than to repeat how sorry I am. There's no question I'll replace the gowns."

She took the chair beside him. "Look on the bright side. We don't have a mad debutante on the loose within Halford Grange."

"No, this is far worse. What if my mother had come in here and you'd been in bed? What if you awoke and startled her? She might have come at you with those scissors."

"Tom, I truly doubt it. She's a gentle soul."

He dropped his hands and looked at her, so many horrible thoughts whirling in his head at once. "She *was* a gentle soul. I don't know what she is anymore."

"She's still the woman who has loved you all her life," Honey said, her hands clasped on her lap.

He wanted to hold her, to touch her, but his mind was in no state to keep him behaving like a gentleman. The last thing he wanted to do was pour his rage and frustration into his kisses, although he sorely needed to kiss Honey just now.

She drew away slightly, no doubt sensing the maelstrom whirling inside him and not wishing to be the recipient of whatever was unleashed. He didn't like to think he'd ever hurt her, but any kiss he gave her now would be rough and demanding against her soft lips. "Will you be all right if I leave you now?"

He was afraid to stay longer. This mix of hot desire and bubbling anger was not anything he'd ever felt before. In truth, he'd never felt less in control in his life.

Honey rose along with him and put a hand on his arm. "Will *you* be all right if you leave now?"

He stared at her hand with such intensity as it rested on his forearm, she quickly drew it away. He laughed bitterly and strode off, for her own sake. Her calm compassion was not what he needed right now. He needed to pound something. It certainly would not be him pounding his body into her innocent flesh.

But damn it to bits, he could not seek his pleasure elsewhere. He was not so far gone as to be ignorant of the repercussions of taking another woman to his bed. Not that he wanted anyone but Honey, and to hell with her damn secret that was preventing them from moving forward.

Why did he need to wait a moment longer to hear it?

How much worse could it be than what she'd seen of his family tonight?

CHAPTER TEN

H ONEY'S FINGERS WERE shaking as she tried to undo the ties of her gown but couldn't seem to manage them all. Sighing, she gave up and decided to simply wear her half-laced gown to sleep. Lottie would freshen it and press the wrinkles out of it tomorrow.

She took off her shoes and stockings and was about to turn down her lamp when she heard a rattle of the doorknob and then a light knock at her door. She'd bolted herself in after Tom had stalked out. She and Belle had faced some very nasty coves trying to steal their Oxford perfume business, but dealing with Tom was almost worse. She'd fallen in love with him, and no matter what happened, whether for the good or the bad, she would never be able to stop loving him.

"Honey, let me in," she heard Tom whisper through her door.

Would it be a mistake? He was a man in turmoil on every front and not in control yet of his quiet rage. But she knew he'd never do anything to hurt her, no matter how wild and unbound his pain.

"All right." If she was completely wrong about him, then she will have learned a harsh lesson. But it would relieve her of the need to reveal her secret to a man she thought she could trust. It would also relieve her of the pain of rejection when he decided she would not make a suitable countess.

But one look at his eyes calmed her at once. He stepped in and closed the door softly behind him, but could not seem to speak yet. She understood the feeling. He had so much that needed to pour out of him, he couldn't get it all out at once. He was still frustrated and angry. Hurt, worried. But what shone brightest in the magnificent depths of his dark green eyes was gentleness and wisdom. "Oh, Tom. Just take me in your arms."

He didn't need coaxing.

He wrapped her in his absorbing embrace, this beautiful way he had of holding her as though he needed to take her into his body and store her in his heart. She felt the same about him. She laughed when he lifted her up against his body and held her close so that her feet no longer touched the ground. He was a big man with a strong, hard body and muscled arms that seemed to have no trouble holding her up.

She wrapped her arms around his neck, and on impulse, pressed her lips to the base of his throat. The gesture broke the dam that was holding him back, and all his feelings spilled out. "Honey, I love you," he whispered and then closed his mouth over hers with a fervor that held no anger, only desire and hope and a promise of forever that she could not hold him to yet because he did not really know who she was.

She had to tell him tonight. "Tom—"

"No words yet, Honey. Give us another moment of just this." He kissed her again, his lips hot and deliciously crushing against hers. He dipped his tongue into her mouth, and she suddenly felt a dozen fiery bursts within her body, like fireworks going off inside her in rapid-fire. It was no longer enough to feel the sensual thrust and tangle in her mouth. She wanted him inside her body.

She felt the hard length of him against her hip and knew he had to be wanting her as badly as she wanted him. His fingers began to work deftly to undo the lacings at the back of her gown and then at her corset. His breaths came faster as he set her down to slip all of it off her, leaving only her chemise.

But that slender scrap of fabric between them appeared to arouse him more than if her body was bared to him. Of course, the eyes made up whatever they could not see, she'd learned that in the book. Tom was probably creating a fantasy in his mind of what he wanted to see rather than what was actually there.

He chuckled as he removed his clothes, leaving only his trousers on. "I know what you're thinking."

"You do?" Oh, he looked like one of those perfectly formed Roman statues, their sculpted, muscular frames simply flawless in design. Was it any wonder women dropped at his feet? How could anyone overlook a big, beautiful body like his?

"That I'm staring at your breasts, trying to see them through your chemise and lusting for what I know lies under there. But I can see them clearly, that sheer fabric hides nothing. I left it on you for the sake of *your* modesty."

"Obviously a false sense of security on my part."

"I'm not going to do anything you're not comfortable with, Honey. This night has stirred so many feelings in me. I expect it has done the same with yours. I won't deny what I want to do with you now. The more I ache, the more I want to bury myself inside you and seek my release." He ran a hand roughly through his hair. "I came in here wanting to take you in anger, not to hurt you but to soothe my own pain. But you have this way of taming me. I can't look at you and keep the rage inside me."

"That's a good thing, isn't it?"

He cast her a melting smile. "Not for an earl who's earned the name Wicked Wycke. It's frightening how much power you have over me. Even more frightening that I just admitted it to you. But there's something in that impudent arch of your brows, the curve of your lips, the sweet pucker of your lips when you are thinking...as you are now."

She returned his smile. "I can't help it. Although I doubt I'm thinking very clearly since we're standing here partly naked, and my heart is in palpitations waiting for you to slip the chemise off me."

"I also came in here wanting to know your secret. Whatever it is, we'll work through it together. I won't abandon you, Honey. I promise."

His words were like a fist gripping her heart and squeezing it hard. "I won't hold you to your word, Tom. I couldn't do that to you. Nor can I tell you yet. Just two more days. Please be patient."

He laughed bitterly. "Patience is the one thing I sorely lack. I'm drowning in stormy seas, and you are the only sane, steady anchor in my life. I don't want to lose you, Honey."

"Nor do I want to lose you."

"Then why hold back?"

She almost gave in but knew it would only add to his dilemma. Adding this problem while he was already trying to sort out his mother's declining health in the midst of a weekend party was not helpful. Also, she feared being overheard by one of his guests. What would happen then? When she shared the secret of her illegitimacy, it had to be to him alone, and they had to be free to discuss it outside of anyone's hearing.

Perhaps he would not see it as a problem, but Tom was not the sort to make rash decisions. He would need time to think about it and be ready to bear the consequences if her secret ever came out. As it was, for an earl of his standing to marry a commoner would cause ripples throughout society. To know she was less than a common-er…would the scandal ever die?

"You're not going to tell me, are you?" He appeared more resigned than angry, but he certainly was not pleased.

"I will tell you, but only once your guests have gone." She met his gaze, looked into his beautiful eyes, and wanted to cry. "Does this mean you're not going to…we're not going to…" She glanced down at her chemise.

"You know so little about men." He removed the pins from her hair and ran his fingers through her curls as they tumbled down her back. Then he drew her forward, cupping the back of her head as he gave her another scorching kiss. And then another. Her chemise had come off somewhere between the string of kisses and his carrying her to bed.

Her heart was pounding through her ears so that she barely heard his intake of breath as they sank onto it together. "You're beautiful, Honey," he said, and then his hands were on her bare skin, big and rough, his touch exquisitely gentle as he cupped her breast, smiling as it filled his palm. He kneaded and teased it, then lowered his mouth and suckled. She gasped and clutched his shoulders, for she was on fire and had never felt anything so powerful before.

His touch.

The feel of his lips and stroke of his tongue across the tips of her breasts was arousing beyond description. But in the next moment, this fire he'd ignited within her turned molten and swept through her arching body.

She tugged on his hair to hold him to her breast.

"Easy, love." He slid his hand downward, caressing her every curve, stroking the inside of her thighs. Ever so slowly, his fingers eased between her folds, sliding in and out, lightly at first, and then with greater speed and pressure, rubbing the pearl of her core until she was mindless and desperately crying out for something more.

Her skin was so sensitive to his touch, sensitive to the rough pads of his fingers caressing and probing her. Sensitive to the light stubble of his day's growth of beard as he nuzzled her neck and suckled the tender spot behind her ear.

Every pulse in her body came alive.

A thousand sensations tore through her at once, like a fire raging out of control. She felt everything. The heat of his skin. The scent of him, clean and bearing hints of bergamot and sandalwood. The arousing weight of his big, hard body atop hers. The gentleness of his touch. The beauty of his sinew and muscle. The soft thickness of his golden hair. The love that shone in his eyes when he looked at her.

She whispered his name.

And held onto him with all her might and all her heart.

He stroked her until she was wild and wanton. He kissed her mouth and throat and breasts, and held her, cherished, in his arms while fiery bursts of pleasure singed her soul and marked her as his forever.

When she'd calmed, he shifted their positions, rolling her atop him. He put his arms around her and began to lightly stroke her hair. "Oh, Tom. I've never felt so wanton in my life."

He kissed her on the forehead. "Just wait."

Her eyes widened. "You mean there's more? Of course, there must be. And you?" She felt him against her hip and realized the pleasure taken had all been hers. "What…" She cleared her throat. "What about you?"

"Not tonight. I'll hurt you if I take you now. I'll…" He emitted a pained laugh. "Don't worry about me. I'll manage for myself. I had better go now."

"Yes, I suppose you must." She nodded. "I love you, Tom."

He kissed her with aching sweetness, then rose from the bed and tossed on his shirt. Wordlessly, he crept from her room.

Only after he'd shut the door behind him did she realize he hadn't responded to her. He hadn't said it back. Did it signify anything?

Or had he just realized he didn't love her?

TOM RETURNED TO his room and stripped out of his clothes, his heart in too much turmoil to fall into an easy sleep. His body ached as well, for he was still aroused and in need of his own release, one he would not take with Honey just yet. A lone moonbeam filtered into the room, providing a thin sliver of stardust glow.

He went to the window and drew his drapes so that his room knew only darkness. He fell into bed and took care of himself, needing that physical release, although it gave him little pleasure. Honey's warm scent was on his skin, and the taste of her was in his mouth. His arms felt empty without her.

He should have told her that he loved her. Yet, she had to know it. They both felt it, this deep recognition that sprang from their souls. The pull on his heart was raw and powerful, the tug for his body to fill hers an agonizing ache.

Two days, he had to keep reminding himself. Soon it would be three. Still, only three days. His guests would all leave on day four. And then what? Would her secret, whatever it was, tear them apart?

He couldn't imagine anything doing so.

He did not manage more than a few hours of sleep before Merrick entered his bedchamber and began fussing about. He drew the drapes, and ghastly sunshine flooded the room. "Damn it, you old hen. Sleeping earl here."

"The Duke of Remson is already awake. His daughter and her friends will be up soon, too. You ought to be there to send them off."

"Telling me what to do now?" Of course, Merrick was right. He cursed as he tossed off his covers and prepared to wash and dress. His first thought was of Honey, but he had no wish to disturb her, especially if she'd finally managed to fall asleep. He'd look for her once Lady Sarah was on her way back to London.

He also needed to look in on his mother. Would she recall anything of last night? Would she remember what she did? He almost hoped she wouldn't because it would horrify her and perhaps terrify her to think she was capable of cutting up Honey's gowns.

Once washed and shaved and dressed presentably, he checked on his mother, but she was still asleep, so he left without disturbing her. Honey was awake, he heard her stirring in her room and heard

Lottie's voice as she tended to her. Would Honey come down to breakfast? He supposed he'd find out soon enough. He wasn't going to knock at her door now.

He went downstairs to see who else was about.

Lord Jameson and his cousin, Lady Phillipa, were seated at the breakfast table along with a few other lords and ladies. Merrick had mentioned that the Duke of Remson ordered his meal and those of his daughter and her friends to be brought up to their rooms. Good, then no one would have to endure their presence this morning. He looked forward to his footmen loading their trunks onto the duke's carriage and was counting the minutes until they left.

As he sauntered to the buffet, he was pleased to see the guests seated around the table were quite relaxed and cheerful as they planned what they were going to do today. He'd arranged for various entertainments, of course. But those would not fill up every hour. The structured activities to keep idle minds busy were no longer necessary now that Lady Sarah and her friends were leaving. They had put everyone on edge with their snappish ways. It came as no surprise to him that not a soul at the table felt a whit of remorse for their absence.

Not even Lord Wrexham seemed put out.

Good, he didn't like to think his friend was a fool when it came to women.

"We're going riding, Wycke," Jameson said, motioning to several other ladies and gentlemen around the table. "Will you join us?"

"Not this morning." He filled his plate and settled into his chair at the head of the table. A footman served him his usual morning coffee. "I had better see Remson safely off."

To his surprise, Honey walked in just then. The gentlemen around the table rose, no doubt thinking what he was thinking. *Beautiful.*

Her gown was simple, a pale brown trimmed with a darker brown ribbon around the sleeves and collar. Not that he cared about the gown other than she looked stunning in it. Her hair was neatly drawn back in a simple twisted bun at the nape of her neck. As he watched her, the familiar ache began to build inside of him.

He'd held her delicious body in his arms last night and needed her in his arms again.

"Good morning, Miss Farthingale," Lady Phillipa cheerfully called to her.

"Good morning." She smiled at everyone. "Please, do sit down. The sausages smell heavenly. I think I must fill up my plate with them."

Tom continued to watch her as she made her way to the buffet. He came to her side. "May I assist you?"

Not that she needed help lifting the lids off the chafing dishes. Nor did he care that the others were grinning at him, for it was obvious he'd taken a liking to her. He glanced at his friends around the table. "I'll have wickets set up for a rousing game of croquet by the time you return from your ride. I know how Lady Phillipa loves this fast-paced sport."

The pretty brunette laughed, for she was full of vigor and considered croquet an old woman's game. "I'm not sure my heart can take such excitement. I think we must play ladies against the gentlemen. It will be so much more fun when we win. What do you think, Miss Farthingale?"

"Sounds perfect. I love a challenge."

Jameson groaned. "Gad, it's no contest. We all know you're going to win, Phillipa."

She sighed. "Only because I can't seem to help myself. I'm always so competitive. It isn't as though I'm that good. No one else cares enough about it, so they just relax and enjoy the game." She turned to the others. "I do hope you don't find me insufferable."

"Not at all," Lord Wrexham assured. "Afterward, I'll challenge you, one on one."

Titters erupted around the table.

Tom exchanged a smile with Honey, who still stood beside him. Yes, beside him was just where he wanted her for always.

Phillipa arched an eyebrow. "You, Wrexham? And you think you can beat me? Very well. What is the winner's prize?"

"A kiss from the loser," he said, earning more giggles from the ladies at the table.

Phillipa laughed as well. "Very well, but the loser must also suffer a punishment. Nothing dire, this is all in good fun."

Tom was enjoying the lighthearted banter, a much-needed relief from last night's tension. "Phillipa, what do you have in mind for poor Wrexham?"

"What makes you so certain Lady Phillipa will beat me?"

Tom chuckled. "Do you seriously believe she won't? You both have horses here. Fine ones. How about loser mucks out the winner's stall?"

Phillipa clapped her hands. "Perfect. My horse has had digestive problems since we got here. Lord Wrexham will have ever so much fun shoveling it out."

Jameson groaned. "Enough, Phillipa. You're ruining my breakfast."

As the others continued to chat and toss jesting barbs at each other, Tom spoke quietly to Honey. "How do you feel this morning?"

She nodded. "I'm fine. And you?"

"Better for having you close," he said and gave her hand a quick caress. "My mother was still asleep when I stopped in before coming downstairs. I didn't want to wake her. I'll go up once Remson and his entourage of peahens leave. The others plan to go riding. Will you go with them?"

"No, I'm not very good on a horse."

"Suits me, then we'll have a little time on our own to read."

Wrexham must have overheard the last remark. "Wycke, am I hearing you right? You're losing your touch, old man. All the two of you plan to do is read?"

Honey blushed furiously, but fortunately, she was facing the chafing dishes, so no one else saw the fire in her cheeks.

Tom casually turned and leaned against the buffet, tossing his friend a grin. "A lot more pleasant than mucking out a stable stall, as you'll be doing within a few short hours."

The others chortled and returned to chatting about their plans for the day.

Tom remained standing beside Honey as she spooned a dollop of eggs onto her plate. Everything about her ravaged his senses. Her lithe, graceful body. The light, vanilla scent of soap that clung to her warm skin. Her smile. Her eyes and the way they glittered like starlight.

However, he dared not say anything more. He'd already been overheard, thankfully caught in an innocent statement. In this, Honey was right. Whatever dreaded secret she had to reveal to him, could not be done while others were around to overhear.

They were on day three of their *closer* acquaintance.

One more day and he'd know the truth.

One more day and he'd ask her to marry him.

She smiled up at him, her expression impudent, or at least appearing so with her eyebrows arched to give her that irreverent look. "Thank you for your assistance, Lord Wycke."

He grinned back. "My pleasure."

She took her plate and settled at the opposite end of the table from him, a stark reminder of their difference in rank. He endured some more good-natured ribbing from his friends when they caught him admiring Honey from a distance.

"Be careful, Miss Farthingale. Lord Wicked still has his eyes on you," one of the gentlemen teased.

One of the other ladies at the table tittered. "He's awfully hard to resist when he turns on the charm."

"Thank you for the warning, Lady Margaret. I shall remain on my guard. I think these handsome gentlemen are all thoroughly wicked, and we must all beware lest we be persuaded to do more with them than read a book."

When they'd all finished, and the others left to change into their riding habits, Tom had a moment alone with Honey. "How are you really?" he asked, frowning in concern.

"Truly, I'm well. I'm not sorry about sharing more than a chaste kiss with you. I'm not sorry about a single moment spent with you. But that discussion is for another time. I was planning on going up to your mother now."

"I'll walk up with you. Remson should have been ready to leave by now, but there's no sign of him yet. I may as well check on her with you before I deal with the duke and his daughter."

They walked up together.

His mother's door was open, and Dora eagerly waved them in. His mother was washed and dressed, now seated in a comfortable chair by the window, which allowed her to gaze onto the garden below. She turned to smile at them as they walked in. "Good morning, Tom. And my dear, Honey. Isn't it a lovely day?"

Tom knelt beside her. "How are you feeling this morning?"

"In very good spirits. And you, my son? What are the planned entertainments for today?"

"Several guests are going out riding, then later, we'll have a few rounds of croquet in the garden. You'll have a grand view from here."

"Honey, will you be playing, too?"

"Yes, Lady Wycke. Our first round will be men against women. Second round will be Lady Phillipa against Lord Wrexham. Loser must muck out a stable stall. We are all hoping that task falls to Lord Wrexham."

"Oh, that does sound fun. Perhaps I'll sit with Lavinia and cheer you ladies on. I'm sorry to turn traitor, my dear boy. But I think you will bear the disappointment with your typical manly grace."

Tom laughed. "I am wounded. My own mother turning against me."

But he smiled in relief, wishing to capture this moment and have her back as she'd always been. Why couldn't she stay this way? Unfortunately, he knew she would be quite different in a few hours. Did she have any inkling of what she'd done to Honey's gowns? Honey, with her typical sweetness, was chatting with her as if last night had never happened.

If only he could be so forgiving.

"What's planned for this evening, Tom?" his mother asked, nudging him out of his musings.

"We'll have music and dancing." He winked at Honey. "I intend to claim two waltzes from Miss Farthingale, if she'll consent."

"Oh, Honey. Please do say yes. It's obvious my son likes you. But watch yourself. He is an irresistible rogue."

Honey cast him a warm look. "Two dances, my lord? That's rather forward of you. But by fortunate coincidence, I happen to have two open on my dance card."

Tom left Honey talking to his mother while he went downstairs to await the duke and his daughter's departure. It didn't take long before they met him in the entry hall. "Wycke," the deflated man said with a shake of his head, "I hope to see you in London. We'll talk further then."

"Of course," he said with a nod. "I wish you a good journey."

He turned to Lady Sarah, who was flanked by her two friends. By the defiant pouts on their faces, he could see they'd learned nothing. Any contrition they might have felt yesterday was completely forgotten.

He was too disgusted to bid them farewell.

"Amelia, Jenna, go on ahead. I'll be right there." Sarah waited for her friends to climb into the ducal carriage before turning to him and flashing him a cold smile. "You'll regret this, Lord Wycke."

He bowed over her hand. "I sincerely doubt it."

"Convey my regards to Miss Farthingale." With a toss of her head, she turned and marched toward her father's waiting carriage.

Disgust and rage filled him once more. He wasn't worried for himself, but that last remark directed at Honey was a threat against her. He would make sure to mention it to the duke when he returned to London. With luck, the man will have shipped his viper of a daughter off to some convent in the wilds of Scotland by then.

He waited until they were through the entry gate to Halford Grange before he turned away to march upstairs. Honey was just leaving his mother's room, and by the warmth of her smile, he knew it had been an excellent visit. "Care to walk along the river with me?" he asked.

She nodded and hiked her gown up slightly to reveal her foot. "I'd love it. I've already put on my sturdy boots."

They walked out together with only the book, and a blanket to spread upon the ground. They wouldn't have long since the riders would only be gone an hour or two at most. But he'd grab any time he could with her. Just having her by his side brought light into his heart.

When they reached the river, he set out the blanket under a shade tree and stretched out atop it, propping on one elbow as he set the book between them and opened it where they'd left off. Honey sat beside him, but she was looking off toward the rushing waters, seemingly lost in her thoughts. "What's on your mind, Honey?"

"That I'm going to miss this place. It's beautiful out here, Tom. I'm glad you made me come here for your weekend party." She shook her head and laughed. "Well, you invited me. My family was going to drag me here whether I wanted to come or not. I was afraid to be here."

"Why?"

She turned to smile at him. "Because I liked you too much already. My meddlesome family knew it and were going to push me at you no matter what my own wishes were. Everything I feared would happen has happened. But I got my kiss from you and so much more. I have no regrets, even though what will come next might be painful for us both."

He reached for her hand. "The only pain will be in our not being together. That isn't going to happen. I won't let it happen."

She leaned forward and kissed him lightly on the lips. "Thank you, Tom. Let's read now. I'm curious to know what binds two people beyond the initial attraction of the senses."

They got through several chapters, one on why arranged marriages often work out when supposed love matches don't. "It's a matter of expectations," he read. "When one enters an arranged marriage, the expectation is low. One's hope is that the partner they are matched with will be pleasant enough to tolerate. When that partner turns out to be tolerable or even more than tolerable, there is relief and acceptance."

"And for love matches?" Honey asked, her eyes luminescent as she smiled at him.

"Too often, the expectations are set high. Often set too high. We expect perfection in our chosen mate and cannot help but be disappointed when he or she fails to meet the ideal we've created in our mind."

"That makes perfect sense. It is one thing to love someone and think they are the most wonderful being on this earth, but it is also important to acknowledge and accept their faults."

Tom nodded. "True love means accepting the person for who they are, not trying to change them into something they cannot be." Was this Honey's secret? Was there was a failing about her that he could not change? If so, it was extremely well hidden. This girl was flawless. Not only in her outward beauty but inside as well.

This was another thing that surprised him, something he now understood after reading the book. He'd noticed Honey months ago because of his low brain response. Luscious body. Beautiful face. Beautiful mane of fiery gold curls. Sparkle in her eyes. Body that stopped his heart. Need to mate with this girl.

While all this still held true, his body's response had quickly turned into something more. Behind the sparkle in her eyes was intelligence and a sharp wit. Behind her smile was gentleness and warmth. Beyond physical lust was the realization of all the other needs she fulfilled. Caring partner. Loyal partner. Loving partner.

He shook out of the thought.

He'd just read this chapter on raised expectations and understood the importance of using common sense, not blind infatuation, before making the leap into marriage. He did not think he was blinded to who Honey was at heart. "Now, onto the chapter about the common threads that connect us to one another."

She inched closer. "Yes, that one has me quite curious. Perhaps this is the most important thing to me. What does an earl descended from one of the most prestigious bloodlines in England have in common with a common shop owner?"

He reached out and caressed her cheek. "What you really want to know is, what will bind us together, keep me from walking away from you once you reveal your secret?"

CHAPTER ELEVEN

HONEY WAS USED to playing croquet with her large and boister-ous family, everyone aiming to strike the other balls into the hinterlands and then grimacing as theirs went flying off the course as well. This match with Tom and his friends was no less rollicking, Phillipa was a one-woman destruction team, her aim always on the mark. She was out for blood now that Lord Wrexham had riled her.

The constant reference to balls had the men snorting and chortling like infants, especially whenever Phillipa threatened to crush their balls, mostly Wrexham's, who at times was rolling on the ground, laughing so hard he could barely catch his breath.

Lavinia and Tom's mother sat together on the veranda, watching them and cheering for the ladies. The sun shone against a brilliant blue sky, and a light breeze swirled around them, carrying the scent of roses from the flower beds.

Nathaniel, Poppy, and Pip had gone for a late ride and now joined Lavinia and Lady Wycke on the sidelines. Periwinkle leaped off Lavinia's lap when he saw Pip and began jumping up and down every time Pip hopped or cheered the men.

When Honey's ball rolled beside Tom's, and she had the oppor-tunity to knock his into the meadow, she hesitated. "Oh, Lord," Phillipa muttered, slapping a hand to her forehead. "Don't go soft on me, Honey. We have to win this game."

Tom winked at her.

His smile was so endearing, she felt herself melting. "I'm so sorry, Lord Wycke. Off to the meadow it must be." She drew back her mallet and suddenly shrieked as he caught her up in his arms and carried her off to the sidelines. "You wretch! That's cheating."

But she was laughing so hard and felt so wonderful held in his arms, she didn't really mind. The game had descended into chaos anyway, and everyone was having too much fun to care who won or lost. Not even Phillipa minded. The real game came next, her one-on-one battle with Lord Wrexham.

He was a handsome fellow, but Honey had thought little of him until now. She couldn't understand why he'd been foolishly pursuing Lady Sarah, and because of it had dismissed him as a dimwit. But he didn't appear to be an idiot at all. She suspected Phillipa would have more of a battle on her hands than she realized. "Tom," she whispered when he brought her a glass of lemonade and came to stand by her side as they watched the game commence. "It doesn't make sense."

"What doesn't?"

"Why was Wrexham fawning over Lady Sarah when he's obviously much more intelligent than to be chasing the likes of her?"

She was surprised when his smile faded, and he stiffened at her side. "Honestly, I don't know. It puzzled me, but who can say what attracts one to another? Look at us. I keep having to remind myself we've only gotten to know each other over this weekend. It feels like you've always been in my life. More important that you always should be in my life."

She nodded. "I hope so. It will be up to you to decide."

"Ah, putting the blame of the outcome all on me?"

She inhaled sharply. "No...I..."

He walked away to see how his mother was faring. By his smile of relief, Honey knew this would be one of her good days. That would cheer him. However, she'd made that stupid remark, tossed the responsibility for their fate all on him, and he would not so easily get over his irritation about it.

She tried to concentrate on the croquet match taking place between Phillipa and Wrexham. Poppy, Nathaniel, and Pip now joined her, and soon afterward, Lord Jameson and Lady Margaret came to stand beside her as well.

Still, she was troubled, not liking the way things had been left with Tom. She resolved to talk to him later to straighten things out. She hadn't meant to dump all responsibility on him. He was not at fault. Nor was she. Circumstances were what they were. Either he'd care and decide not to see her again, or he wouldn't care, and they'd marry.

Had she told him before they had shared this weekend together, she was certain he would have walked away. He might still, but at least she'd given it her all. If they were meant to be together, then they would be.

She returned her attention to the field of play and cheered along with the ladies for Phillipa. The men rooted for Wrexham, calling out advice and warnings to him, usually when he was about to take his shot. "The dignity of our manhood is at stake! Don't fail us."

However, no one was surprised when he lost.

Nathaniel covered Pip's eyes when Wrexham then gave Phillipa a kiss hot enough to set fire to the lawn. Grinning from ear to ear, he then removed his jacket, rolled up his shirt sleeves, and sauntered to the stable. "Wait for me!" Phillipa hurried after him.

Lord Jameson groaned. "After the kiss he gave my cousin, I'd better go chaperone them."

"I'll come with you," Lady Margaret said.

Poppy laughed softly. "I think all four of them need chaperones. Ah, Lady Margaret's father is thinking the same thing. He's going to join them in the stable. Oh, poor Margaret. I do hope she gets one stolen kiss from Lord Jameson. She obviously likes him."

"I don't know what all the fuss is about," Pip said.

Nathaniel ruffled his hair. "You will in time."

Lunch was a pleasant affair, and Honey could see Tom relax as his mother joined them at the table, seeming to have an easy time chatting with her old friends. In truth, she did well at first. But Honey noticed the moment she began to fade and stumble over her words. Poppy and Lavinia also began to notice, and they all did their best to take over the conversation and keep her from growing agitated.

When everyone rose from the table, Honey came over to her. "Lady Wycke, may I help you upstairs?"

Poppy joined them, leaving Nathaniel and Pip to assist Lavinia, whose mind was sharp as a tack but whose legs were not what they used to be. "Yes," Poppy said, "we've had a busy morning. I think we ought to rest for the afternoon. We want to be at our best for this evening's dancing."

Lady Wycke glanced around nervously. "Where's my Tom?"

Honey felt Tom's presence but was afraid to turn around and look at him. He was still irritated with her. "He's right behind us, Lady Wycke. See? He'll join us once he's attended to your guests."

She nodded and was docile as a lamb as they brought her upstairs.

Honey felt Tom's gaze on them the entire time, felt his heartbreak, and his frustration like a heavy hand upon her shoulder. When they reached Lady Wycke's bedchamber, Dora and one of the Halford maids were there to assist her. "Thank you, Lady Poppy. Miss Farthingale," Dora said. "I'm glad she had a lovely morning."

Honey smiled at her. "So are we."

She turned to Poppy when they were once more in the hall. "Will you be retiring as well?"

Poppy shook her head. "I'm meeting Pip in the library. He's going to choose a book, and we're going to read. Speaking of books…"

Honey groaned. "I don't want to talk about *that* book."

"Why not? I saw you reading it with Lord Wycke by the river. How are things progressing between the two of you?"

"I don't know." She hadn't shared her secret with Poppy, although she wasn't afraid her cousin would ever betray a confidence. But Poppy's sister, Violet, knew. And their cousin, Holly, knew. Two Braydens, Finn and Joshua, knew because they'd been there when the secret was discovered. She did not want it going any further.

Poppy arched an eyebrow. "You don't know? The man is obviously in love with you. He can't keep his eyes off you, and his expression softens every time he glances your way."

"Well, perhaps. But we've only known each other a few days. You knew Nathaniel all of your life. It took years for him to realize he'd loved you all along."

Poppy hugged her. "You're right. I'll stop meddling now. Which you know is very hard for a Farthingale to do. Oh, Honey. You know I only wish the best for you."

"I do." She gave her a hug in return. "I'll be fine. No matter what happens. People will start leaving tomorrow. I just want to enjoy this evening and as much of tomorrow as possible. It's best not to make too much of one weekend. We'll see what happens once we're all back in London."

"Well, I see you as right for each other. Not that my opinion accounts for much, but I watched him when he courted Nathaniel's sister. No spark. No light in his eyes. Not even a flicker. However, with you? He lights up like a blazing torch."

Honey passed an off-handed remark to dismiss further talk of Tom. Since she was feeling restless, she decided to go for a walk. She grabbed a light shawl from her bedchamber and strode out of the house, past the garden, and toward the meadow. Her destination was the river. The trail that ran alongside it was a very pretty one, and she hadn't explored very much of it.

Her footsteps fell silently upon the soft earth. The ground would soon be covered with leaves as the seasons changed, but right now, the trees were still lush and brimming with life. A few squirrels darted across her path and skittered up one of the trees. Birds called to each other with noisy chirps from among the branches.

She hadn't walked far before she spotted someone seated on a fallen log, his back turned to her as he stared at the rushing water. He seemed to be studying the water's flow, the way it struck the protruding rocks along the riverbed and tossed spumes of white spray into the air. The spray formed a mist around the man, the foamy tendrils twisting over the water and reaching out to envelop everything upon the nearby shore.

She recognized Tom as he rose, his golden hair shining in the sunlight, his broad shoulders and muscled arms seemingly broader against the lawn fabric of his shirt. The mist still swirled around his boots, but now that he was standing, she saw he'd tossed aside his jacket and cravat, no doubt wishing to get comfortable while out here on his own, lost in his thoughts.

He drew nearer to the edge of the water. He was still watching the flowing current and had not noticed her yet. She remained where she was, studying him.

Yes, this is how she would remember him, this big, handsome man standing amid nature, lost in contemplation. His wise and soulful eyes taking all of it in.

The butterflies in her belly began to flutter, and her heartbeat quickened. She loved this man. How could she let him go? Why would she not fight for him? He'd been telling her all along how he wanted her by his side. He'd felt it deep and raw inside of him, this instinctive, primordial understanding they were meant for each other.

And what had she done to fight for their love?

Absolutely nothing.

She'd told him the decision was all on him. No wonder he'd left her abruptly earlier, unhappy she'd tossed this burden onto his shoulders. If she wanted his heart, she had to do everything possible to keep them bound in love. She could not simply tell him she was of illegitimate birth and then sit there meek as a mouse awaiting his decision.

Of course, she had to tell him the truth.

But she also had to do whatever was necessary to convince him none of it mattered. Only their hearts mattered. Their love for each other would see them through the worst life had to throw at them.

Who were the elite of society to tell them what to do or how to behave? What made any of them more worthy? Her thoughts immediately turned to Lady Sarah and her toady friends. Were they better than her because they were born to privilege?

Never. They were odious young women.

Tom, sensing her presence, turned suddenly toward her.

The fiery look in his eyes left her breathless.

Oh, this man.

He captivated her with his dark intensity. She felt his frustration and savage need as though it was a living, breathing thing between them. She held her own breath as he wordlessly strode toward her out of the mist.

Seemingly out of the mists of time, for this is how eternally she felt bound to him.

Wasn't this how she'd always hoped it would be? The man of her dreams walking toward her just like this? She thought of the flower, love-in-a-mist. She'd spoken of it to Tom on her first day here.

And now he was marching toward her, that dangerous gleam in his eyes and pain etched in his face. She ached to be swept into his arms, needed to be held by him, and kissed by him until he possessed all that she held and all that she was.

"Honey," was all he said before swallowing her in his arms and lifting her up against his tense, hard chest. Then he was kissing her, his mouth warm and urgent on hers, possessive and hungry. Devouring her. Taking all of her into his heart.

He kissed her again.

He kissed her on the neck, nibbling at her ear.

He kissed her at the base of her throat.

Her heart was pounding so wildly, she could hardly catch her breath. "I love you, Tom. I'm so sorry about what I said earlier. I didn't mean it to sound as though I didn't care."

"I know." He kissed her again, his lips claiming hers with conquering fervor, once more long and deep and infinite. He did not let go of her when he ended the kiss, nor did she have any desire to let go of his body. Her legs had turned to butter and would never hold her up.

A smile quirked at the corners of his lips, but it was a wry, sad one. "I wasn't angry with you. Never with you. Everything hit me in that moment, and you took the brunt of it."

"Still, I shouldn't have said it as I did."

"You could have said nothing, and I would have behaved the way I did. I was watching the game, enjoying the light breeze and the sun on my shoulders. Enjoying you standing beside me. Everyone was having a good time. I noticed the older ladies in the distance, Lavinia and my mother laughing heartily. That precise instant in time was too perfect. But this is how it had been while I was growing up. I wanted our life to be like this again."

He kissed the top of her head and continued. "Then I thought of Sarah and her viper's tongue. She means to hurt you. How, I don't know. I looked up and saw my mother's eyes begin to take on that lost look and knew she would soon be gone from us again. She barely made it through luncheon."

"And while all that was going through your head, I thoughtlessly piled the burden of my secret on you."

"The not knowing what you are hiding burns in my soul," he said with a wry laugh. "I've found you, and I don't want to let you go."

"Oh, Tom. I'm truly sorry." She shook her head. "I'll tell you now if you must hear it and cannot wait another day. I was being selfish, wanting to wring every last drop of this magical time with you, wanting to share two dances with you tonight. Waltzes no less."

She glanced up at him. "I was afraid of the way you would look at me once you knew. I'm still afraid, but I'm not ashamed of who I am. I hope you won't be either."

He led her over to the fallen log and sat her down beside him. There was something calming about the *whoosh* of water and intimacy to the swirling mist.

"Tell me, Honey. Whatever you say to me, no matter the outcome, your secret will never leave my lips. I promise. I know how important this is to you."

She nodded.

Closing her eyes tightly, she told him everything. "My parents were not married when they had me. That is, they thought they were, but my mother had married another man when she was very young. Then she was told her first husband had died. She had no cause to doubt the news. In truth, his family and hers truly believed it and mourned his loss. A few years later, she met and married my father."

He ran a hand roughly through his hair. "Oh, Lord. But said *first* husband wasn't dead?"

"That's right. No one realized it...at least, I don't know if and when they did. His death was announced in the papers a little over a year ago. Our parents tried to hide the truth from Belle and me, but we found out. So, you see, if you were to marry me, you'd be marrying...you'd be..." She sighed. "I cannot even say aloud what I am."

A bastard.

Tom shook his head and uttered a muffled curse. "Society will certainly see you that way. Those like Lady Sarah, brainless, heartless, and mindless, will go out of their way to humiliate you."

"They will do their worst, I know. But they can't hurt me. I don't care what they think of me. I know who I am and am proud of what I've made of myself. However, you were raised in society. These are your friends. These are the men you will have to face in the House of

Lords and the women who will cut you from their elite circle because of me. Will the men who sit on the board of your clubs now terminate your membership? What of your own servants? What will they think of you when they learn that I am beneath them?"

"Are you trying to talk me out of marrying you?"

Her eyes rounded in horror as she stared at him aghast. "No, never! I hope you know I want to marry you with all my heart and soul. I love you for the man you are, Tom. The thought I might not be with you has me dying inside. I love *you*. I don't care about your title. I don't even know how wealthy you are, not that I care about that either."

He shook his head. "Then you are the only girl in England who doesn't."

"Truly, I don't. It's obvious you have a beautiful estate, and I cannot imagine you being reckless with it or any of your other holdings. My family runs a successful business, and we have some wealth of our own. Probably nothing close to yours, but our perfume shops and the lotions, soaps, colognes, perfumes, and other products we sell are more than enough to support us comfortably. That is another thing. Can you accept that I will continue to help out in the family business? We don't have to speak of it now. I just want you to think about it." She folded her hands on her lap, another thought coming to mind. "It was your eyes."

"What?"

"I fell in love with them," she said, speaking into her lap.

He tipped her chin up so that she met his gaze. "You fell in love with my eyes?"

"Yes. More precisely, I fell in love with the man I saw behind them. I didn't know who you were when I first noticed you. But I saw intelligence, compassion, wit in them. I saw honor and valor. I began to think of you as the man with intelligent eyes. You were gorgeous, too. But everyone saw that in you." She smiled at him. "I don't wish to sound like a low-brain female, especially since females are only supposed to have that one, higher-level brain, but I will admit to having heart flutters over you. Your body is hard to overlook."

He laughed. "Good to know I wasn't the only one hopelessly lusting."

"Every woman lusted over you. But I liked to think of myself as more than a mercenary debutante out to catch herself a wealthy, titled husband. You were perfect. Lord Intelligent Eyes. Then you had to make that stupid wager with Joshua Brayden."

"That?" He winced. "How could I pass it up? It was the easiest twenty pounds I ever made. All you Farthingale girls are named after flowers. How could he think your name would be anything other than Honeysuckle?"

"Ugh! Don't even say it aloud."

His eyes gleamed with affection. "I thought myself safe, even though you were stunning and my heart shot into my throat every time I saw you. Still, I was sure I could not take a girl by the name of Honeysuckle Farthingale seriously. No danger to my state of bachelorhood."

She punched his shoulder lightly but wasn't really angry with him. She simply detested the name. How could her parents have done this to her? It was almost as bad as the secret of her birth. "Do not call me that!"

He raised his hands in mock surrender. "It didn't take me long to realize I'd fallen in love with you. We'd hardly exchanged two words in greeting, and I knew. Beautiful and clever. But so much more than that."

"Beautiful, clever, and illegitimate." She folded her hands on her lap again and stared down once again. "I don't want to lose you, Tom. You now know everything about me. This is why I didn't want to tell you before tomorrow. I don't think I could bear to see disgust in your eyes...those eyes I fell in love with."

She rose. "I'll leave you alone to think about what I've said. I'm sorry if I've added to your burdens."

He took her hand and held her back gently. "You spoke of my eyes. I'm not certain I'm all that much smarter than the next man. However, I was born with an innate understanding of human nature and a certain clarity in judging others. It is hard to fall in love with someone when all you see reflected in their eyes is a balance sheet tallying up your wealth. Every girl I've ever met has had that look, except you."

He rose to stand beside her. "Just as you fell in love with my eyes, I fell in love with yours. Every time I looked at you, I saw spirit, wit, extraordinary compassion. You've shown it all along to my mother, who is obviously helpless and fading."

He caressed her cheek. "What I've never seen is that mercenary balance sheet. What I've never seen is cruelty out of you. The other night, I wanted to take you by the shoulders and shake you because you were so forgiving of what my mother did to your gowns."

"She didn't understand what she was doing."

"I know. It still made me angry." He sighed and walked toward the river's edge. "This discussion has made me realize something."

She joined him. "What?"

"I've spent the past month worried about what others might think about my mother's condition. I didn't want them laughing at her. But I also didn't want them laughing at me. Perhaps this is what really concerned me most, that I would be ridiculed and thought of as lesser because of her." He released a long, ragged breath. "What a dolt I've been. Who gives a rat's arse what others think? They're the fools if they find cause to taunt and ridicule. Anyone of worth would never behave this way."

"Bravo, my lord!"

"What about you, Honey?"

She shook her head in confusion. "What about me?"

"I don't need time to think about what you've told me. Nothing will change the way I feel about you. It took honor and courage to tell me this before you'd trapped me in marriage."

"I would never keep such a thing from you. This is why I had to tell you now."

"And this is why my choice is easy. Beautiful, clever, and trustworthy. I'll never know a moment's doubt with you. A life with you in it will always be a happy one for me. If your secret ever came out…most secrets do, it's only a matter of time before it does. But if it ever came out, I will be no less proud to call you my wife."

He took her hand and kissed her softly on her trembling palm. "Miss Honeysuckle Farthingale, and I promise never to call you that again. But this is important, so, my dearest Miss Farthingale, will you marry me?"

CHAPTER TWELVE

"WHAT?" HONEY SAID, shaking her head as though she hadn't heard right.

Tom smiled and kissed her on the wrist this time. "Will…you…marry…me?"

As his words penetrated her brain, she threw her arms around his neck, holding him so tightly, he felt the breath rush out of him. But he quickly recovered and was about to laugh when he realized she was sobbing. "Sweetheart, why the tears?"

He knew what she was feeling, the burden she'd been carrying in her innocent heart ever since learning the circumstances surrounding her birth. And Honey, being Honey, could not conceive of holding back the truth from the man she loved and wanted to marry.

"Blessed saints, I love you." He wrapped his arms around her slender body and held her in the protective circle of his arms as every ounce of pain, vulnerability, and a thousand other desperate feelings poured out of her.

But he also saw the sparkle of relief in her eyes as she said, "I love you, too."

"I know." He kissed her tear-stained cheeks, not really needing an answer to why she was crying. She'd tried to deal with her secret as only an innocent would, by declaring she did not ever wish to marry. This is why she was always running from him, running away from the one man she knew could force her to shatter that pledge.

No wonder he'd been so confused whenever he was around her. He felt awful about it now, for all the while he'd thought she was playing a coquettish game to capture his attention, her heart was breaking.

"I know," he repeated in a whisper as the flood of tears continued to pour out of her. She loved him. She'd loved him from the moment they'd met. She'd loved him from afar.

But that's all it had taken for him to fall in love with her, as well.

A mere glance from afar.

He'd first spotted her at one of those London society affairs, the crush of guests disappearing as his eyes trained on this lovely, ethereal innocent. Indeed, at first sight, he thought he must have been dreaming, she was so beautiful. Here he was now, holding her in his arms and never wanting to let her go.

And why ever should he? What was he really giving up to have her? Absolutely nothing if her secret remained safe among the handful who knew.

But secrets always had a way of coming out. He didn't care for himself. He only cared that Honey's feelings would be hurt. As for those in society who would ridicule and shun her? He didn't care to mingle with them anyway.

Cutting off relations with the likes of Lady Sarah and her toady friends was no loss.

"Honey, do you think you can stop crying now?"

She shook her head. "Not yet. I need another moment."

"All right, love." She was still holding onto him like a barnacle clinging to the hull of a sailing ship. "May I take your tears as acceptance of my offer? Or do you need longer to decide?"

"I know what is in my heart." She laughed through her tears. "I know what has always been there for you. Yes, Tom. Yes, I will accept your offer, with all my soul and being."

"Well, isn't that something," he said softly and released her to run a hand roughly through his hair. "I'm to be a married man."

He could not stop grinning.

Nor could she, as she took out her handkerchief and dried her tears. "And I'm to be married after all. To the man with the kind, intelligent eyes. To the best man in all of England."

"Shall we announce it to our guests?"

She took his arm as they strolled back toward the house, and a feeling of warmth permeated his body. This was one of the things he loved most, this feeling of rightness whenever she walked alongside him. "Would you mind if we didn't just yet? I'd like my sister and parents to hear it first. There's no doubt my father will give his permission. He'll probably leap at you and hug you as tightly as I did just now," she said with a laugh. "If you wish, we can quietly tell Poppy and Nathaniel. And your mother, of course."

"No," he said with a slight frown. "Not my mother yet. I'm not sure what she'll blurt if we tell her now. Let's wait until we announce it to your family."

"As you wish. Sadly, I suppose you're right."

"My sister is going to beat me about the head when she learns of this. She'll be thrilled, no doubt. But to learn I married you after only a weekend's acquaintance, after the agony I put her and Malcolm through...well, my little sister is never going to let me forget it."

Honey's rich laughter filled the air. "My family will be in an up-roar, a happy uproar. I made such a fuss about not coming here, and an even bigger fuss about never marrying." She leaned her head against his arm. "But Belle had given me *The Book of Love* and was convinced I was destined for the altar no matter what I did with that book."

She began to nibble her lip as they now walked in silence across the meadow and into the back garden. "Tom," she said after a moment, "do you think it's possible? Do you think the book is magical?"

He shrugged. "I don't know. It didn't make me fall in love with you. I was already in love with you before you ever set your hands on the book. But reading it certainly helped me understand what I was thinking and feeling, and what you were thinking and feeling as well. Perhaps it did work some magic in bringing us around to admit how we felt about each other."

She nodded. "And to understand what a precious thing it is to find true love."

"What will happen next with the book? It gets passed around from debutante to debutante, doesn't it? Who will you pass it on to next?"

She rolled her eyes. "I don't know. Obviously, one of my three Yorkshire cousins. Holly, Dahlia, and Heather are down here for their come-outs. Well, not Holly. She's widowed, and even though she's hardly older than me, she refuses to put herself on the marriage mart again. I suppose the book will point me in the right direction when the time comes."

They strolled through the garden in no particular hurry to enter the house. "Violet told me that once she had married Romulus, she was going to give it to me. But then an odd feeling suddenly came over her, and she had to give the book to Belle. As for Belle's decision when it came her turn to give it away, her choice was easy. She refused to listen to a word I'd said and insisted on handing me the book."

"I'm grateful to her then." He grinned. "If not for your sister, you might still be running, and I might still be chasing."

She cast him a wistful gaze. "And at some point, you would have given up and stopped."

He nodded. "It would have taken quite a while. I can be stubborn when I want something, and I wanted you badly."

When they returned to the house, tea was being served in the drawing room. Although he and Honey said nothing to the others, Tom did not think anyone could overlook the hot, steaming glances he kept tossing her.

They all had to know something was in the offing.

Well, they would learn of it soon enough.

He intended to break the news to both families immediately upon their return to London and marry Honey as soon as possible thereafter. Why wait to wed? He already ached for her. How many nights had he spent alone in his bed, his thoughts and fantasies about her? No, there would be no delay in getting her to the alter.

He hadn't discussed it with her but did not think she would mind. Once a decision was made, he liked to act quickly. Announce the betrothal. Arrange for the special license. Draw up the betrothal contract...or that could be done later, he didn't care. Marry her before the week was out.

His thoughts turned to his sister, and he knew missing their wedding would disappoint her greatly. But he hoped Anne would understand. Caithness was in the upper Highlands. It would take a fortnight for word to reach her. And then having to wait perhaps another month for her to arrive in London? It was just too long to bear.

Of course, she would understand. She and Malcolm hadn't been able to keep their hands off each other. He felt the same way about Honey. They would know exactly what was going through his mind and why the need for haste.

He could hardly wait an hour, much less an entire week. To hold off beyond that would be impossible, for he'd seen Honey's body and knew the taste, the silken touch and scent of her, and the mere thought of it made his heart pound and the blood rush to his head.

No, he was helpless when it came to the girl. He would never have the strength to keep his hands off her.

Perhaps tonight, if she had no objections. After all, they would be husband and wife within the week, less time if he had his way.

Tom did not know how they made it through the tea hour and

later, the supper hour without everyone guessing they were betrothed. Then again, most of the younger ladies and gentlemen were here for precisely the same reason, to make matches.

After supper, the dancing started. It was not considered good form to open with a waltz, but Tom could not wait a moment longer to hold Honey in his arms.

No one minded when they realized he'd broken with protocol.

Wrexham had a wicked grin on his face and was ogling Lady Phillipa. *Good luck with that.* Phillipa was no meek maid. But she was a decent girl, and Wrexham wasn't getting anything from her without a proposal of marriage.

Lady Margaret had her eyes on Lord Jameson, blushing with glee when he claimed her for the dance.

The elders had their eyes on all of them, the fathers knowing what the men wanted from their precious, innocent daughters, and the mothers holding their breaths that an offer of marriage might spring forth this weekend.

Tom walked over to Honey, who was seated beside Lavinia and Poppy. Periwinkle, as ever, was perched on Lavinia's lap, his little ears perked as he sniffed every lord and lady who drew close. "I believe this dance is mine, Miss Farthingale."

He held out his hand.

She put hers in his and smiled. "It is, my lord."

While this small party was far less grand than a London affair, it was the last night his guests would be here, so everyone had rested, bathed, and dressed in their finery for this evening's festivities.

He'd fallen so hard for Honey it was no surprise she took his breath away. She always did, never more so now. "You look beautiful."

Starlight shone in her eyes, and it pleased him to see her this happy, the haunting sadness completely gone. "Thank you."

He discreetly nuzzled her neck. "Vanilla soap."

She nodded and then cleared her throat. "Tom…"

"Yes, love," he whispered as they waited for the musicians to strike the first notes.

A blush dotted her cheeks. "Will you come to my room tonight?"

Hell, yes.

But he wasn't going to force her. "Do you want me to?"

The fire in her cheeks was response enough. He chuckled. "I'll be there."

Although he was pleased, it also pained him to know Honey was wearing a borrowed gown. Poppy had loaned it to her knowing his mother had destroyed Honey's two evening gowns. Fortunately, the cousins were close in size and build. He doubted anyone would ever guess the pale lavender silk hadn't been made especially for her.

He felt a shiver run through her body when he placed one hand at the small of her back and took her other in his hand. "Ready, love?"

She nodded.

As the first strains of the waltz filled the room, he drew her closer and twirled her in a circle, following the arc of steps and turns along with their other friends. But his attention was on her, as he feared it would always be, even into their dotage. Well, it wasn't a fear so much as a deep, abiding joy to know this was the woman who would share his life.

She, however, was looking with wide-eyed glee at Wrexham and Phillipa.

Tom could not hold back a chuckle. "Oh, lord. She's trying to lead."

Neither could Honey hold back her laughter. "They're going to fall atop each other unless one of them gives an inch."

"Wrexham will win this one. He has to, or else she'll have his nuts in the cruncher for the rest of their lives."

Her eyes widened. "Tom!"

Perhaps he had been a little too descriptive, but she was to blame for that. He was never on his guard around her. He could be himself. "Sorry," he said with a smirk, knowing by her own struggle to suppress a laugh she wasn't really offended. "They'll sort it out. Do you realize I've never danced the waltz with you before tonight?"

She nodded. "You probably tried to ask me. But at every society event, I spent half the night sneaking peeks at you and the other half running away from you. I'm glad there's no need for that anymore."

"No wonder I could never find you."

She regarded him earnestly. "No hiding from you ever again."

He wanted to kiss her.

When did he not?

Later that night, in the wee hours of the morning, once everyone else had retired to bed, Tom quietly knocked at Honey's door. When she opened it to let him in, he saw that she had changed out of her gown and wore only a thin nightrail. He smiled, liking that she'd taken the pins from her hair and left it unbound. He had changed out of his formal attire and tossed on the plainer trousers and shirt he always wore whenever working on Halford Grange.

He stepped in and shut the door behind him, his heart giving a tug when he saw Honey's expression. Love mingled with trepidation. Giving herself to a man was not something she'd ever done before. Yet, she wanted to give herself to him because she loved him. "Honey, we can wait for this until we are husband and wife."

"Do you not wish to—"

He laughed softly. "I wish to so badly, I think my spleen is about to rupture."

That brought a smile to her face. "So do I. But, I was afraid you'd think less of me if we…coupled…before we were wed."

"I wouldn't. We are only days away from a ceremony that would only make official what is already in my heart."

She let out a breath. "I feel the same. Take me to bed, Tom."

He lifted her in his arms and set her on the mattress but made no immediate move to take the nightgown off her. He stretched out beside her, still clothed, and took her back in his arms, just holding her and stroking his hand along her arm.

He kissed her on the forehead, still sensing her uncertainty. But this was Honey, and this was why he loved her. She had a well-defined code of honor and was struggling with herself to do the right thing. It was ironic really, for when she held out no hope of ever being married, she would have given herself to him without hesitation.

But now that they were about to be married, she wasn't certain. It meant something to her to come to their wedding bed unspoiled.

Hell. If this was important to her, he'd wait until they'd had their ceremony.

Truly ironic, the only debutante he wanted was the only one ever to resist him. "I suppose my spleen can hold out for a few more days," he joked.

Perhaps it was his willingness to wait, not to force her into doing something she might regret, that seemed to decide it for her. "Tom," she whispered and tried to take off his shirt.

Lord, it would take hours if her fumbling was any indication.

He helped her by removing it himself. "Are you sure, love?"

She nodded. "I just needed a little time to feel comfortable with it. Not that I ever had a moment's doubt about you. Or any doubt about us. But I didn't know if I was giving up a special moment…our wedding night, if we…you know, did this sooner. However, you're what makes it special, and that won't change."

She nudged him onto his back and shifted her body so that she lay almost atop him, her soft, plump breasts resting against his chest. She reached up and brought her lips to his, her kiss light and gentle. He felt the delicate warmth of her hand on his shoulder, then almost shot off the bed when she slid it lower, down his chest, down his stomach, and lower still.

He took over at that point, knowing she'd made her decision.

Perhaps next time, he'd work the nightgown off her with more finesse, but right now, he just wanted it off her, no impediment to his view of her beautiful body.

He'd seen her, touched her before. Even so, he inhaled sharply when he removed the flimsy obstruction and had an unhampered view of her firm, creamy breasts. Ah, how they sent his low brain into spasms.

He loved the way her molten curls cascaded down to her hips.

Truly, this girl took his breath away.

Fire roared through his veins. He rolled her under him, hardly able to hold a rational thought as he initiated this mating dance as old as time itself. He kissed her on the mouth, his lips molding to their lush fullness. At the same time, he cupped her breast, kneading it lightly and swirling his thumb over its dusky rose tip.

She licked her lips, and her breaths came a little faster now. He liked the way her body arched toward him as she responded to his touch and responded to the heat and weight of him as he positioned himself atop her.

But he took the brunt of his weight onto his elbows, careful not to crush her as he dipped his head and took the rosy tip of her breast into his mouth, suckling and licking until it tightened. She clutched his head, her fingers twining in his hair.

Blessed saints.

He had no intention of removing his mouth from the creamy mound unless it was to shift to the other, which he now did and received a breathy moan of satisfaction in response. He felt her skin warming, saw the light flush in her cheeks, and knew it was time to stoke the fire. He slipped his hand between her legs and touched her sweet core, taking only a few gentle strokes before he felt her became slick.

"Tom," she whispered, her hands still grasping his head.

"I know, love." She was so soft and sweet that he couldn't get enough of her. She was so beautifully aroused, so open in her purrs of pleasure. But this time, he wanted to share in the pleasure, feel her responsive shudders as he joined with her.

He drew away a moment to remove his trousers, and there was no question he was ready to claim her. Her eyes were still closed, and perhaps it was for the best this first time. "Sweetheart, this might feel a bit tight at first. The discomfort won't last."

She nodded and opened her eyes to smile at him.

He positioned himself between her legs and eased himself into her slowly, pushing in only a little at a time. Even so, the feel of her tight innocence against his tip had his control unraveling. In truth, shattered. All mindfulness abandoned as primordial urges sprang from somewhere deep within the hidden corners of his heart. He did not think, he only felt.

Hunger. I want this girl.

Possession. Need to mate with her. She is mine.

Craving. I can't get enough of her. She is in my soul.

His thrusts became more urgent as her tension eased, but this was new to her, and although she was slick, she still fit him like a tight sheathe. The friction, the steadily undulating motion of their joined bodies, the thrusts in and out, were at the same time exhilarating and unbearable. Well, he could bear it. Of course, he could bear the mounting pressure, that slow burn soon to result in a volcanic eruption. He felt the molten heat in his blood, felt it flowing like liquid fire through his every pore and limb.

He quietly roared when the burst came, spilling himself into Honey, driving himself deeply into her until he was spent of every drop. Possessive pride filled him, for he'd also heard her gentle cries of pleasure mingled with his grunts and roars, and knew they'd reached their fiery ecstasy together.

He was reluctant to pull out, but she had drained him, and they couldn't remain like this, still joined and him crushing her with his big, sweating body. He finally did ease out of her and wrapped her in his arms, holding her in his enveloping embrace.

This is what he had been missing. This is what his heart, soul, and body had lacked until now. Everything felt different with her. Better. Timeless. She had the ability to turn him into a ravenous beast, and at the same time, had tamed him so completely. "How do you feel, my love?"

She smiled at him. "Must I say it? Can you not see the happiness on my face?"

"Yes, I do see it." Because Honey could hide nothing from him.

There was no one like this girl.

How was he going to manage the next few days without her?

"How do you feel, Tom?"

He rolled onto his back and groaned, a moment later reaching for her hand and entwining her fingers with his.

He brought her hand to his lips and gave it a soft, lingering kiss.

Words failed him.

How could he describe this moment of idyllic bliss?

CHAPTER THIRTEEN

H ONEY FELT TOM stir from her bed shortly before daybreak.
Oh, heavens! What they'd done!

She turned to look at him as he quietly tossed on his trousers and shirt, admiring his lean, muscled form in the graying light. He must have sensed her watching, for he smiled as his gaze met hers. "I didn't mean to wake you."

His arms had been around her, holding her through the night. She'd felt a chill when he rose to dress. "I was awake."

He came around to her side of the bed and sat down, his weight causing the mattress to tip and roll her toward him. He took advantage of her nearness to kiss her lightly on the lips. "How do you feel?"

"Different. A little overwhelmed." Perhaps this was not what he'd hoped to hear, but everything did feel different this morning. She drew the covers over her bosom for the sake of modesty, feeling not quite as bold or wanton as she had a few hours ago.

"I love you, Honey." He frowned lightly. "Have your feelings for me changed?"

"Yes," she said, throwing her arms around his neck. "They've deepened. Turned into something so much more. I didn't think it possible, because I already loved you so much."

He laughed and kissed her on the cheek. "It's hit me much the same."

"Truly?"

He put his arms around her and began to run his fingers lightly through her hair, seeming not to mind as the long strands spilled over his forearm. "In my university years, I was a bit of a hound. My wicked reputation lingers to this day, most of the gossip false. I've long ago stopped feeling the need to...pollinate every flower I come across."

She snorted. "Sorry. Is that what you were doing? Pollinating me?"

He gave a chuckling groan. "I'm trying to be polite here. Are you in any doubt about what I was doing?"

She shook her head, knowing her smile was still impertinent. She *eeped* when he suddenly drew her onto his lap. The sheet had slipped off her chest and was barely hiding anything of her body now. She tried to shift in order to wrap it more securely around herself, but he did not appear to be inclined to help.

He dipped his head and kissed the swell of her breast. "As soon as we are back in London, I'll obtain the special license. Every organ in my body will rupture if I have to wait beyond tomorrow to call you my wife. What I felt last night...I truly don't know how to describe this intensity of feeling. Despite my years of experience, nothing prepared me for it. I knew I loved you. But last night...our coupling...added an entirely new aspect."

She nodded. "The book called it a shared intimacy. One of the many threads that connect us."

He caressed her cheek. "All I want to do is roll you back under me and keep *connecting* us until we are wrapped up tight in our own cocoon. No point waiting even another day to obtain the special license. I'll go right now."

"And abandon your other guests?" She laughed. "Now I've learned something new about you. You are most impatient when you're starved for sex."

"Only with you, love. Only ever with you." He kissed her on the lips and sighed as he eased her off his lap. "Nathaniel will bludgeon me if he finds me in here. He and Poppy trusted me to behave myself."

She winced. "They trusted me, too."

He rose to hunt for her nightrail that had been tossed aside in haste last night. He found it lodged in a rumpled ball between the mattress and the footboard. "Here, sweetheart. Put this on, or I'll never have the strength to leave."

Honey quickly donned it, but the thin cotton was no substitute for Tom's warm body. "Yes, do go. Poor Lottie. She'll shriek if she finds you in here."

"Blessed saints, even when you're covered up, I can't resist you."

She gave a mirthful gasp and held up her hand when he started toward her again. "Oh, no. Get out of here, my wicked lord. The entire household will be stirring soon."

Once he was gone, she made up the bed, straightening it just enough to make it look slept in by one person. Right now, it looked as though a jousting match had taken place on it. She also opened her window to allow in the cool, autumn air.

The scent of sandalwood, his scent, was on the bed and in the room. Probably on her skin as well. She washed reluctantly. But she had to. It wouldn't do for his servants to know she had been with him outside of marriage.

Her respectability was already in question because of the circumstances surrounding her birth.

She inhaled lightly.

Goodness! She hadn't given it a thought last night when asking him to join her in bed. What must he think of her? Illegitimate and wanton.

But she knew he thought no such thing, and this made her love him all the more.

She was washed and dressed by the time Lottie came up to draw her curtains aside to wake her. "Oh, Miss Honey. You're up bright and early."

She nodded. "Most of Lord Wycke's guests are leaving today. I thought I'd rise early to wish them a good journey. Some have quite a distance to go. They might have taken off already."

"Yes, a few have. Most will leave right after breakfast. But you're to stay until tomorrow and return to London with his lordship and Lady Wycke, is that not right, Miss Honey?" She glanced around as though the wall might have ears and whispered. "It isn't my place to say, but he seems quite taken with you."

She could have denied it or merely shrugged and claimed she hadn't noticed. But Lottie, although not book smart, was sharp when it came to people. Also, she was a terrible liar, and Lottie would know it at once. "I'm quite taken with him, too."

That seemed to please the young maid to no end. "We all could tell by the way he looked at you whenever he thought no one was watching. No one important, that is. We could see it, but we're just his staff, here to serve his lordship. A good maid ought to be invisible to her betters. So, we go about our jobs, unseen."

Honey frowned. "But your good work is noticed. This house is beautifully maintained, and none of us has lacked for anything throughout our stay. That's a tribute to all of you. I planned to thank Mrs. Finch personally."

"Oh, she'll be thrilled. Few guests think to praise her. They simply partake of all that's offered and then just take themselves off."

"I understand how much effort it takes to make things run smoothly."

Lottie nodded. "Miss, shall I style your hair?"

"Yes, please do." She sat on a chair by the window, listening to the girl chatter while she fussed with her hair, first drawing it back and braiding it, then twisting the braid in a fashionable knot at the nape of her neck. A few, curling wisps framed her face.

"There, Miss Honey. Don't you look lovely?"

"Thank you, Lottie." Although the hour was still early, she decided to stop in next door to see how Lady Wycke had fared. She had been too tired to join in the festivities last night. The door was slightly ajar, so she nudged it open a little more and peeked inside.

Oh, dear.

Dora and the maid assigned to tend Tom's mother were both at her side, trying to calm her. "He'll be right back, m'lady. Have a cup of tea, won't you? He'll pop his head in by the time you've finished it."

"Why are you lying to me? I know he's gone. Where is he?"

Honey's heart sank as she heard the poor woman utter this often-repeated refrain. She'd heard it often over the course of the weekend. "Where's Tom? Where's my Tom?"

Honey ran to Tom's door and knocked on it. "Lord Wycke, are you in there?"

His valet, Merrick, appeared. "May I help you, Miss Farthingale?"

"It's his mother. She is asking for him." She began to wring her hands. Tom's valet slept in a side room off the earl's elegantly appointed quarters. Did he know where Tom had been last night? Not that he would ever comment upon it if he did. But heat crept into her cheeks anyway. She hoped he would attribute it to concern over Lady Wycke. "She's quite agitated. I think he ought to come right away."

His expression turned to one of worry. "I believe his lordship is in the dining room. I shall fetch him at once."

"Thank you. In the meanwhile, I'll see if I can do anything to help her." She ran back to the dowager's quarters but did not know what she could possibly do if Dora and the maid had failed. Still, she had to try.

She approached quietly and drew up a chair beside her. "Lady Wycke, what is the matter? Is there something I can get for you?"

Her eyes had narrowed, her pupils darting back and forth in an attempt to keep her gaze on all of them at once. There was a slightly frightening aspect to her look, as though she saw them as people who meant to do her harm.

Honey wanted to take her hand but dared not. "Ah, I see you have several books on your night table. May I read you one of them?"

She pulled one off the pile and opened it without awaiting her answer. "Oh, this is one of the legends of King Arthur. I do enjoy these stories. Do you remember the wizard, Merlin? And young Arthur pulling the sword out of the stone?"

Tom's mother was still eyeing her suspiciously.

She began to read anyway but hadn't gotten beyond the first page when his mother interrupted. "You were with my Tom last night. I heard you."

Her eyes rounded in horror, and her breath caught. "I...I..."

Dora and the maid came to her defense, no doubt believing the woman was referring to Tom's father, who was long since dead. "Nonsense, m'lady," the maid said. "You're quite mistaken. This is Miss Farthingale. Lady Poppy's cousin. She doesn't know your husband."

Dora chimed in. "Your son had a party last night. What you heard was music and chatter. Everyone had a lovely time."

Tom strode into the room and knelt before his mother. "What's the matter, my darling?"

Relief washed over her. "There you are, Tom. Where have you been?"

Honey's stomach twisted in a knot when she saw the pain in his eyes. "Downstairs. Our guests are leaving today. I must see them off."

His mother struggled to rise from her bed. "Oh, I ought to be by your side."

He didn't look pleased, but he nodded. "Yes, if you feel up to it. They'll understand if you aren't."

She seemed confused, as though she'd already forgotten why she'd risen. "No, no. Where's my tea? My bones are aching, and I'm feeling quite poorly today."

Tom took her aged, shaking hand. "Dora will pour you a cup. I'll come see you again in a little while. As soon as our guests are safely on their way."

He tried to rise, but she wouldn't let go of him. "Promise me."

He gave her hand an affectionate squeeze. "I will."

"Because I must speak to you about our son. He's brought a...Cyprian...into our home. I will not have it. He was with her last night. I heard them."

Honey wanted to crawl into a hiding hole and never come out.

Tom was much cooler about it than she ever could be. "I can assure you, there is no Cyprian under this roof."

Dora was ashen. "Oh, Lord Wycke. I don't know what's got into her today. She's never been this bad. First accusing sweet Miss Farthingale of entertaining your father in her room and now accusing you of bringing a woman of ill repute into this house. She isn't well."

"I'll come back and spend a little time with her once our guests are gone. Do what you can, Dora. I know this isn't easy for you or any of us. Miss Farthingale," he said, offering her his arm. "Come down to breakfast. You must be hungry as well as overset."

She nodded and allowed him to guide her out of the room. "Oh, Tom," she whispered. "She *heard* us. I'm so ashamed."

"For what we did last night?" His expression darkened.

"I don't regret it. But now everyone thinks she's delusional when we know she isn't."

He placed a comforting hand over hers. "She is, Honey. She mistakes me for my father. She believes he's still alive. As we walked out, you heard her talking about my sister and the big man who stole her away. Malcolm MacLauren. He is Anne's husband. Just as you will soon be my wife."

She knew he was right, but it still gnawed at her insides, particularly because she was sensitive to her birth circumstances. Illegitimate and wanton. Could she overlook the scandal if the truth of either was ever found out?

More important, could Tom overlook the scandal?

CHAPTER FOURTEEN

H ONEY KNEW THE return trip to London would not be an easy one for Tom or for herself. His mother had not been well since yesterday morning. This was unusual and troubling. Until now, there had always been moments in the day when Lady Wycke had been her old self, cheerful and charming. To lose even that had all of them worried, and Tom most of all.

The sky was overcast, matching the pall over their hearts as they all climbed in the carriage for the journey back to town. Even though it was not raining, Tom had chosen to ride in the carriage with them.

Honey knew at once it was a mistake, for she could see he was in quiet torment.

He was a man used to being in charge and in control, able to fix things as soon as they broke. But he could not fix his mother's fading luster.

Their only moment of joy since yesterday had been when they'd told Poppy and Nathaniel of their betrothal. Poppy had hugged her and said, "I knew it. I'd hoped for it. May you be as happy as Nathaniel and I."

Nathaniel had expressed similar sentiments.

This was the last time she'd seen Tom smile, and she could see that he was now straining within the confines of the carriage, no doubt feeling it was more of a tomb than an elegant conveyance. "Lord Wycke, I think you ought to ride your horse the rest of the way."

He cast her a wry smile. "Looking to be rid of me already, Miss Farthingale?"

"Yes, my lord." She arched an eyebrow impudently. "You are too big and are hogging all the space. I'm squeezed into a corner."

He knew she was teasing him. "Very well, I shall do so after our next stop."

That stop came soon afterward when they drew into the courtyard of the Four Roses Inn. The innkeeper and his wife hurried out to greet them. Tom hopped down and arranged for a private dining room, ordering a hearty meal for all of them even though the hour was still early.

A moment later, he helped her down the carriage steps. "You are the only debutante in London who would object to my proximity," he whispered, keeping hold of her far longer than necessary and surely catching the notice of anyone watching.

She cupped his cheek, only a brief touch before she drew her hand away. "No objection, my lord. As you well know, considering our...proximity the other night. I can't bear to see you in pain. You were suffocating in the carriage and tormenting yourself."

He sighed as he released her. "I thought my presence would help."

"Ride alongside the carriage when we resume the journey. She'll see you, and it will comfort her just as much as if you were seated beside her. Truly, there is nothing any of us can do at the moment. But I will ask my uncle, do you know him? George Farthingale? He's a brilliant doctor. There may be nothing he can do for your mother's condition, either. But he can help us to understand what is going on, and what we can do to comfort her best."

"We? I like the sound of that." His smile was no longer mirthless.

Honey breathed a sigh of relief, noting a trace of lightness in his eyes that had been dulled by worry until now. The situation was not a happy one, but knowing they would deal with whatever came next together took a weight off his shoulders.

They helped Dora and his mother down and settled them in the private room. Once tea and apricot tarts had been set out for them to nibble while waiting for their meal, Tom offered her his arm. "Walk with me?"

She nodded, for both of them needed a dose of fresh air.

They strolled to the edge of the garden marked by a stone wall. Tom leaned against it and folded his arms over his chest as he faced her. "I'm trying to keep my mind off her, but it's impossible. She's deteriorating so rapidly. It's hard to believe only a few months ago she was herself, perhaps a little forgetful and dithering. But nothing like this."

"Her scattered thoughts might have been going on longer than you know, only she was able to hide it until now."

He cast her a wistful smile. "You would have picked up on the cues immediately. I ignored and denied them. I think this is another difference between men and women. You nurture, and we fight. But how does one fight an invisible enemy? You can't pound it with your fists. You can't fight it with a weapon."

"You can only lend comfort and assistance when needed."

"Ha! In this, I would likely earn failing marks. I'm impatient. Need to get things done and see the results come to fruition. Sitting helplessly by a bedside is not something I can do for more than a few minutes."

"That's because you view it as being helpless. But it is a huge relief for the person who is in need of comfort. It isn't about you. It's about them."

He chuckled. "Nathaniel often remarks that Poppy has the sweetest way of kicking his arse to the Antipodes and back. I think you have that same quality, politely telling me I'm an arse, and I should get over my own petty gripes."

"Oh, Tom. They aren't petty. Just misguided."

He leaned forward and kissed her lightly on the lips. "Have I asked you to marry me yet, Miss Farthingale? Just want to be sure I have because I am never letting you get away. This is another thing I realized the book spoke about. Connections. These threads we weave that bind us over time. We aren't weaving the same threads. My colors will be different from yours. But put together, they create the beautiful tapestry of our life."

"You are waxing poetic."

"Hardly." He leaned forward and stole another kiss. "But I'm noticing that your strengths are perfectly compatible with my weaknesses."

"Just as your strengths are a good match for my weaknesses." She took his arm when they turned back toward the dining room. "*The Book of Love* says it is our brains that make these connections, but I'm not certain I agree. We knew it, felt it before we'd ever spoken to each other. Our hearts were drawn together. Perhaps this was the unconscious part of our brain already at work and gathering all these bits of information in the blink of an eye and sending it to our heart."

He opened the door to lead her back inside the inn. "Like an officious, but very efficient clerk checking off a list. Ah, here's a girl. Let's see what we like about her. Beautiful smile. *Stamp*. Glittering eyes. *Stamp*. Stunning body. *Stamp, stamp, stamp*. Because that's worth three. Charming voice. Clever, too. Every line now stamped. Ah, this one. Move her along to his heart. Damn lazy organ. About time it awoke."

Honey laughed. "Oh, yes. I'm sure it is exactly like that."

He smiled at her with great affection, but she had her hand on his arm and felt his tension return as they drew nearer to their table.

Honey sat beside Lady Wycke. Dora sat on her other side. They ate, helped Lady Wycke with her meal, the task slow and clearly beyond Tom's patience, but their talk had helped, and he did not appear quite as tortured as before.

When they reached London, Tom ordered his driver to stop at his townhouse to drop his mother and Dora first. Honey waited while he took a moment to settle her in her quarters and alert his staff. Within fifteen minutes, he'd accomplished what he needed and strode back out. "Give me another moment," he said, leading his horse to the mews behind his home to hand him over to one of the grooms who took care of the row of stables.

He returned quickly and hopped in the carriage with her. "I hope you don't mind. I wanted to be free to talk to your aunt and uncle about our plans. You'll want to let your sister know, of course."

She laughed. "All of London will know of our betrothal within a matter of minutes."

"Right, that." He arched an eyebrow. "Do you think we might ask them to keep it quiet. Just spread the news among the family. Our betrothal will last only a few hours. I would like us married by tomorrow."

"You've been saying this, but I didn't realize you meant it. Why the rush?" She chuckled. "Other than the fear your spleen will explode if you must wait longer to have me in your bed."

"Isn't it reason enough? Why must I deprive myself of your nurturing arms?" His expression turned serious a moment later. "If my mother should...pass...before we are married, it could be months before we can hold even a quiet ceremony. Besides my obvious lusting desires, I am concerned about this secret of yours. If it ever should get out, I want us facing the gossip and ensuing scandal together as husband and wife. My name and title will offer you protection. If anyone dares offend you, they will have to deal with me."

She nodded, but fear for herself was one of the lesser reasons. She wanted to do this because she loved him, and he needed her beside him at this particular moment. Also, they'd coupled, and although it was unlikely that one mere night would lead to her conceiving a child, it was quite possible.

If they had to wait to marry and she began to show... Tom did not need more scandal attached to his name. "Poor, Aunt Sophie. Perhaps one of my Yorkshire cousins will have a traditional ceremony instead of the rushed, patched up affairs that have become the standard for Farthingale weddings lately."

"Perhaps, but where would be the fun in that? I think I'd dash my head against the wall if I had to endure a year of wedding planning. And wait a year to get the woman I loved into my bed? Having to wait even one more night is an impossible task."

Fortunately, Honey's aunt and uncle were at home when their carriage arrived on Chipping Way. Tom barely had time to hand her down before Farthingales began to emerge from every house on their side of the quiet street. "Oh, no," she moaned, knowing they would never have privacy now.

Honey's sister, Belle, and their cousin, Violet, tore out from Number One, Chipping Way. "What a coincidence," Violet said, giving Honey a hug. "Your sister just happened to be visiting me when we noticed Lord Wycke's carriage roll down the street."

Of course, it was utter rubbish. They knew she was returning today. They must have had their noses to the window for hours waiting for just this *coincidental* moment.

Her cousin, Laurel, and Lady Dayne appeared, too. "I just happened to be visiting Graelem's grandmother when—"

"When you happened to notice Lord Wycke's carriage," Honey said with a laugh, grinning at Lady Dayne, who hadn't moved that fast in as long as Honey could remember.

"Yes, how did you know?" Laurel hugged her.

More cousins trickled out of Number Three, as well as the Farthingale patriarch and matriarch, John and Sophie. Honey turned to Tom in dismay. "So much for a quiet moment."

He did not seem at all put out. "As I mentioned when we started the journey, my life has been too dull lately. Since everyone is conveniently here, we may as well make the announcement."

Her eyes widened in alarm. "No, Tom. They can't keep secrets."

Her Uncle John groaned. "Tom, is it?"

Honey blushed.

Tom shook his outstretched hand. "Yes, sir. I plan to obtain the special license today and marry Honey tomorrow."

One would think the queen had come to tea there was such a fuss made. But after the initial squeals, shrieks, and hugs were done, Honey followed her aunt, uncle, and Tom into her uncle's study. But before entering, she turned to her sister and cousins with a frown. "Please keep this quiet. I'll explain later, but word must not spread beyond the family."

She held out little hope, for her family was too large. Also considered within that definition were the families of their husbands. Camerons, Braydens, Emorys, and Daynes. Their circle numbered in the hundreds.

"I'm coming in with you," Belle said. "Sisterly privilege. You can't keep me out."

"Very well." She wasn't going to win this argument, nor did she really mind having Belle by her side since they'd both been damaged by their parents' horrid secret, and she knew how much Belle worried over her.

Her aunt and uncle hadn't been told their secret, nor did she wish to tell them now. Perhaps it wasn't fair to keep them in the dark, for they'd been nothing but generous with the entire family and were going to host her wedding.

But she wanted to bury the painful secret in the deepest recesses of her mind and quickly forget it.

She entered the study behind Belle and closed the door. They both took seats beside her aunt on the tufted leather sofa. Tom remained standing next to her. "Is there a reason for this...haste?" her uncle asked, assuming the chair behind his desk.

"Yes, but it has to do with my mother's health. She isn't well. Honey will tell you more about it later."

Her aunt cast him a sympathetic gaze. "Oh, I'm so sorry, Lord Wycke."

"Thank you." He nodded. "It is something I will need to consult your brother about, Mr. Farthingale. I've heard of George, of course. He's very well respected. I ought to have called him in sooner, but she didn't seem to be that bad at first. This weekend was a terrible strain. I hate to think I worsened matters by bringing her to our country estate."

"George will be stopping by shortly. Have a drink with us in the meanwhile, and we'll discuss these wedding arrangements. Since Honey's parents are in Oxford and you feel certain there is no time to spare, I'll act on their behalf."

"And I'll ring for Pruitt to roll in a cart," Sophie said. "You must be hungry, as well, after your journey." After summoning the family butler, she sat back down and took Honey's hand. "I've had more hastily planned ceremonies here than I can count. That is, unless you prefer to hold the wedding elsewhere, my lord."

"No, I'd be indebted if you took over the planning and made all the arrangements, Mrs. Farthingale. Charge all the expenses to me. I insist on it. You are doing me an enormous favor. I'd be at a loss where to even start. Just tell me where and when to show up. I'll be there."

"Tomorrow, you say?"

Honey nodded, "If Lord Wycke can obtain the special license."

"I'll get it today, no worries. Having one of the oldest titles in England has its privileges."

Her aunt smiled. "You'll have your wedding tomorrow, my dear. Late afternoon, if that is all right with both of you." She shot to her feet. "Mrs. Mayhew will have my head for this. She and her poor maids will have their work cut out for them."

Belle rose as well. "Let me know if there's anything you need. Finn and I will help. That is, our cook and the rest of our staff will assist yours. We can send over maids and footmen. Scullery maids. Our larder is fully stocked because we've had to do quite a bit of entertaining recently. I think Finn will go into hiding if he has to sit through yet another dinner party with those stodgy aristocrats. But you are obviously the best of them, Lord Wycke." She gave him a heartfelt hug. "Truly, the best of men."

She followed Sophie out of the study, the two of them already chattering about logistical plans for the hastily organized affair.

Honey rose and turned to Tom. "I had better go help them, too. I'll leave you gentlemen to discuss the betrothal details and will let Pruitt know to send Uncle George to you as soon as he arrives." She turned on her heels. "Belle, wait!"

Then she turned back and threw herself into Tom's arms. "You truly are the best of men. I love you." She gasped, realizing she'd let that slip in front of her uncle. "Oh."

Tom laughed and kissed her on the cheek. "I love you, too. I'm sure your uncle figured as much the moment my carriage rolled onto Chipping Way to first pick you up."

Her uncle ran a hand through his hair. "Sophie knew. Women have a way of sensing these things. I just try to keep my head low and hide in my study whenever I can. Well, congratulations to the pair of you. My lord, I doubt you have any idea what you are getting into by marrying into this family. As chaotic as it may appear, all I can say is that you will know happiness beyond measure."

Tom was still smiling at her as he said, "I know, Mr. Farthingale. I felt it the moment I set eyes on her. Ours is a love match."

Her uncle chuckled. "I suspected as much. You have that brains-turned-to-pudding look about you."

Honey's eyes widened in surprise. "Uncle John!"

"Lord Wycke knows this is true. Am I not the worst offender? Your aunt has had my heart from the moment I first set eyes on her. I'd climb mountains on the moon for her. So, I know the feeling very well."

"Oh, dear," Honey teased. "My uncle will drive a hard bargain over the betrothal contract now that he realizes how much you love me. Stand firm. Do not give away more than is reasonable."

"Get out of here, Honey," her uncle said with mock severity. "I hope you are a better negotiator when it comes to your perfume products."

She laughed. "Of course, I am. I don't love my dealers and distributors anywhere near as much as I love Lord Wycke. Although there was a charming older gentleman at Harrington's—"

"Out!" he said with a grin. "I promise not to fleece him…not too badly."

Honey told Pruitt about sending Uncle George to the study and was still smiling as she made her way to the kitchen when one of her cousins stopped her. Holly was her widowed cousin, only a few months older, but she'd tragically lost her husband.

Honey felt a twinge of remorse that she should be so happy when Holly had to be feeling the loss of her love. "I was going to help Aunt Sophie and Belle in planning the wedding breakfast," Honey said. "It will really be more of a wedding supper since we're marrying in the afternoon. I hope this will not be too difficult for you."

"You marrying and I having lost a husband? Nonsense." Holly gave her a hug. "I'm so happy for you. I will admit, I first thought Joshua Brayden was meant for you until you spoke Lord Wycke's name. I heard the slight melt in your voice and saw how your eyes lit up."

"Oh, dear. Was I that obvious?"

"Yes, but only to me. I doubt Belle or my sisters picked up on the nuances. I assume he knows the secret."

Honey nodded.

"I was sure you'd tell him before allowing him to propose to you. He must be an excellent man."

"Yes, he is quite wonderful."

"Of course, he is. Or else you wouldn't be marrying him." Holly pursed her lips. "I think Joshua would have married you if you hadn't found Lord Wycke. These Braydens are quite honorable. And protective of those they love. Finn certainly was when it came to Belle. Joshua has those same protective instincts. It's rather nice, really. But don't tell him I said so, or he'll be even more insufferable than he is already."

Honey stifled a smile. Her cousin, who was never getting married again, had just mentioned Joshua Brayden three times in less than a minute. Well, if that wasn't a sign of who should get *The Book of Love* next, she didn't know what was. "Shall we see if we can help Aunt Sophie?"

Holly nodded. "I'd love to. Mine wasn't much of a wedding. But yours will be the loveliest. Violet's ceremony was held right here in the garden. Yours will be as well, I imagine. It's the perfect spot. In the sunshine, surrounded by flowers. Shaded by graceful trees. Loving family all around you. I wish I'd had that."

Honey held her breath, for Holly had never spoken of her wedding or the loss of her husband until now.

"My wedding took place in the midst of a downpour. My gown was soaked by the time we entered the church. My sisters had helped me fashion my hair, but it was a wet jumble as I stood beside the altar and pledged my heart. His family wasn't pleased. His mother and father refused to attend at first. But they did, quite reluctantly. Neither of them cracked a smile or shed a single joyful tear throughout the ceremony."

"Oh, Holly! I'm so sorry."

Her cousin shook her head as though to dismiss those unpleasant memories. "No, don't be. I was young and foolish. Perhaps I should have taken the torrential rain as a bad omen. But it does not diminish my happiness for you. For all of my cousins who have found true love."

She locked her arm in Honey's. "Aunt Sophie can work miracles in under a day, but I'm sure she'll be glad for our help."

Oh, Holly was definitely getting *The Book of Love* next.

Could the signs be any clearer?

CHAPTER FIFTEEN

T HE DAY WAS filled with sunshine and a light, warm breeze blew through the garden as Honey stood beside Tom under a bower of roses, struggling to hold back her tears of joy. "You look beautiful," he said, smiling down at her.

She was dressed in a pale yellow silk gown and had jeweled pins in the shape of honeysuckle flowers in her hair that had been swept back in a gentle wave and intricately braided in a twist at the back.

He looked magnificent, his love reflected in the splendid green pools of his eyes and in the affectionate smile that would not leave his face.

She heard sniffles and knew her cousins were crying happy tears for her.

Since Lily was still in town, she was able to be here for the wedding, along with her husband, Ewan, and his grandfather, the powerful Duke of Lotheil. Seated beside the crusty duke was Ewan's dog, Jasper.

As the ceremony began, Jasper trotted over to Tom and remained quietly beside him throughout their exchange of vows. Tom gave Jasper a quick scratch behind the ears to acknowledge him and made no move to nudge him away.

Honey lost her struggle to hold back tears. It was as though Jasper knew Tom needed someone by his side. When the minister tried to shoo him away, Honey stopped him. "No. He's family."

This day was a happy one for both of them, but she knew their happiness could not be complete. Tom's mother had not recovered. It turned out that her Uncle George, a man capable of working medical miracles, could do little to help her.

For this reason, there would be no grand tour for their honeymoon.

They would return to the Wycke townhouse this evening, not even one night spent away. She had insisted on it, although perhaps it wasn't all that wise. Even though the earl's quarters were quite separate and apart from the rest of the bedrooms, it was not far enough away to allow Tom to forget his burdens and responsibilities.

Yet, how could they travel now?

"Do you, Honeysuckle Farthingale, take..."

Oh, drat! Did the minister have to shout her name for one and all to hear? "I do," she said, casting the poor man a murderous frown.

Tom chuckled.

So did her sister and cousins.

Jasper wagged his tail, and his breathy, drooling pants sounded remarkably like laughter as well. She sighed. *"Et tu, Jasper?"*

Everyone in the family adored the loveable sheepdog, never more so than now. He would not leave Tom's side throughout the entire wedding celebration, as though knowing Tom had no one else with him. Not his sister, not his mother, and not any cousins who were spread all over England and could not possibly reach London in time.

But Tom had Jasper.

Somehow, his well-behaved presence made everything all right.

As the hour grew late, they returned to Tom's house...hers now, too. She offered no resistance when he swept her into his arms and carried her over the threshold once his butler opened the door to them. "Good evening, my lord. My lady."

"Good evening, Winwood." He strode past the man and marched up the stairs with her still in his arms.

"What will your staff think?" she whispered in his ear.

He kissed her cheek. "That I am a man in love with his wife. Shocking, isn't it?"

She sighed. "Goodness, I just realized."

He paused as he was about to open the door to his bedchamber. "What, love?"

"You're an earl."

He strode in and shoved the door closed with his shoulder. "So I've been told."

"That means I am a countess. Your countess." Her eyes widened in surprise. "So foolish of me not to have thought about it sooner. I mean, I knew it. This was the entire reason I fretted about telling you my secret. When you decided the circumstances of my birth were not important, your status flew out of my mind. I simply did not think about it again until just now. Our son will be a little viscount, assuming we have a son. And assuming you give him the courtesy title. I'll have Belle create a new perfume. We'll call it A Night With An Earl. Too long a name, do you think? Perhaps Earl's Temptation."

"Getting a little ahead of yourself, aren't you? On the perfume and the son. We don't have our little viscount yet. Although I promise to do my duty with uncompromising diligence and zeal to make it come about."

She arched an eyebrow. "I don't doubt it. Look at us. I think we are both panting harder than Jasper ever was today. I will admit, I'm excited at the prospect of tossing off our clothes and climbing into bed."

He set her down only long enough to help her remove her gown and undergarments. He unpinned her hair and gave her a naughty prelude as he kissed along her thighs when removing her stockings. "Tom!"

"Lord, you're sweet." He removed his boots and clothes, tossing them off with all haste and very little care.

They didn't walk so much as tumble onto their marriage bed,

groping and kissing each other as they did so. Honey's heart was pounding wildly. She clutched his shoulders, her fingers hungrily curling into his thick, corded muscles, her body straining toward his and rubbing against him as he settled over her, for she now understood the wonder of this passion she felt for him.

He kissed her on the mouth with ravenous abandon, his kisses deep and probing. Then he moved lower to kiss her neck, her shoulder, and finally her breasts. First one, then the other. Teasing and suckling, his touch fiery and exquisite. He eased his hand lower to prepare her for his intimate entrance, but she was already hot and eager for him.

Their joining was an untamed thing, urgent and intense. He was fully embedded in her, holding her in his arms in that absorbing, swallow-you-up way, as though he wanted to take her inside of him and etch the taste and touch of her skin in his memory forever.

His movements were powerful and graceful, carrying her along on waves of fire.

She studied his face, the beautiful, masculine artistry of it, the fine angles, and chiseled features. His eyes gleamed like dark, fiery emeralds. His body was a finely honed work of art as well, exquisitely hard and muscled.

She felt the same volcanic build she'd experienced the first time, the same divine pressure mounting and fire in her blood. He knew just how to arouse sensations hidden deep within her, sensations that could only be awakened by his touch. "Tom," she cried softly as a thousand bursts of pleasure coursed through her body all at once.

He must have been holding himself back, seeking to pleasure her before he took his own, for she soon felt his shudders and the liquid throb and pulse of his release.

She held him back when he eased out of her and attempted to draw away. "I love you."

"Blessed saints, I love you, too. Let me up, sweetheart, before I crush you."

"You aren't hurting me. You feel so good against me."

"So do you." He kissed her brow. "Let me hold you in my arms."

She edged closer as he stretched on his back and made room for her to burrow against his chest. His arm curled around her, and he began to stroke her lightly along her hip. "This is nice, Tom."

"Very."

"I like that we no longer have to hide from others, that we can be together whenever we want and for as long as we want. Do you think forever is long enough?"

He chuckled. "Not nearly enough."

For Honey, the best part came with the morning sun, knowing she was waking to find Tom beside her. She was tucked in his arms, her back against his front. His body was hot, which served to keep her warm.

She'd never managed to put on her nightgown. In truth, she had no idea where it had landed. The last she saw of it was last night at the foot of her bed, just before they'd gone at it like feral animals.

She turned and placed her hand to his cheek, feeling the rough stubble of his face. His hair was slightly rumpled, but on him, it looked quite appealing. "Good morning, my lord."

"Morning, my lady. You're as beautiful as a sunrise." He shifted her under him and made love to her again, this time slowly and with an aching tenderness that made her love him all the more.

It was almost noon by the time they finally rose from their bed and readied themselves for the day. Of course, no one required or expected them to leave the earl's quarters, but in this, she and Tom were of a similar nature, unable to laze about all day in bed.

Her clothes had been moved into the adjoining bedchamber that served as her quarters now that she was countess. But this was more for the sake of her lady's maid and his valet in completing their duties. It wouldn't do for Mary, her new maid, to be dressing her while Tom strutted around half-dressed. Nor could she traipse around in her nightgown while Merrick was attending to Tom.

However, the nights were for her and Tom to share in the one bed. Neither of them wished to sleep apart. Ever.

"Shall we look in on your mother?" she asked after they'd gone downstairs and taken a light repast. But she immediately saw he was reluctant. "I'll run up and see her," she said. "I'll send for you if there's any change in her condition. She's well settled here and diligently cared for. We can take a few days to enjoy our newly wedded bliss. Shall we go out today?"

He smiled at her. "I believe I owe you a dozen new gowns. How about I take you to your modiste, and afterward, we can take a ride in the park or go wherever else you'd like."

"That sounds perfect."

Lady Wycke was sleeping when Honey entered her quarters. "How is she doing today, Dora?"

"Oh, my lady. Not very well. She's hardly opened her eyes. She hasn't touched her breakfast."

Honey frowned. "Does she have a fever?"

"No, my lady," said one of the attendants her uncle had sent over after examining Lady Wycke the other day. Her name was Alice, and the other attendant was Frances. They were sisters in their mid-thirties, with a gentle manner about them.

"His lordship and I will be out for a few hours. We'll look in on her when we return."

"She may do better in the afternoon," Frances said. "I'm sure she will."

Honey returned downstairs and found Tom seated behind his desk in his study. He was looking over some documents but set them aside and cast her a tense smile when she walked in. "How is she?"

"Sleeping. She's in good hands. Shall we go for our ride?"

"Yes, I'm eager to get out. But shopping first."

She rolled her eyes. "Only three gowns were damaged this past weekend. Madame de Bressard knows my size and has the fabrics and patterns. I need only send word to have her duplicate them."

"You'll need a new wardrobe now that we're married and you are my countess. Those charming gowns you wore as a debutante—"

"Won't do now that I am no longer innocent?"

Laughing, he rose and took her in his arms. "Don't put words in my mouth. Can a husband not spoil the wife he adores?"

"Well, put that way. Yes, he may. It will make Madame de Bressard very happy."

"And you, love?"

She kissed him. "You are what makes me happy."

"Well, that tears it. Now you shall have me completely wrapped around your little finger. I'll be worse than any of those besotted husbands I used to mock."

"Poor you. How the mighty have fallen." She kissed him again and put her arm in his. "Come on, let's go."

They stopped first at her modiste and spent a good hour selecting a dozen new gowns and matching accessories for her. "Would you mind if we stopped at some of the men's shops next?" she asked, thinking only to check on the supply of the colognes and soaps she regularly sold the London merchants.

But this was a discussion they'd neglected in the midst of their courtship and hasty marriage. "Tom, we haven't spoken of my role in my family's perfume business. Belle and I have been more involved in it these past few years. And now with my father's injured leg and the nastiness that went on at our Oxford shops this past summer, he needs our help more than ever."

He frowned. "We'll need to talk about this. But this conversation is better held among the four of us. You, me, Belle, and Finn. It is also something to be discussed with your parents. We'd planned on visiting them soon anyway. Oxford is not so far. We can go up any time."

She nodded. "Yes, we ought to make plans for it after we talk to Belle and Finn. He's had her write down the formulas for all our fragrances and will keep them locked away for safekeeping. They're quite valuable, the lifeblood of our business. I think my parents can take care of stocking our Oxford shops. We have three so far, but honestly, the town cannot support more than that. We were thinking of expanding into London, no longer merely supplying other shops, but opening our own."

"Let's discuss it with Finn and your sister. He's the financial wizard. I'm sure he and Belle have spoken of this already."

"I think we must also invite my cousin, Rose, and her husband, Julian."

"The viscount?"

She nodded. "Do you know him? He seems to have no problem having his wife run a thriving business. In truth, I would love to know how she manages her responsibilities as a mother to their children, a viscountess, devoted wife, and a businesswoman. Would you mind if we had them over for supper tomorrow night as well?"

"I think it's an excellent idea."

"We ought to have spoken of this before we married. I don't know why I didn't pursue it when you first proposed to me. Perhaps because I wanted you more than anything in the world. I love what I do, but I love you more. If I were forced to give up something, it would not be you."

He grunted. "I felt the same. I wanted you and knew we'd work the rest of it out. The one thing I could not compromise on was marrying you. Would you mind waiting a couple more days before stopping in at the men's shops? Also, our marriage isn't common knowledge yet. The announcement hasn't come out yet in the papers."

"Oh, yes. We ought to put it in soon." She glanced at him. "You're frowning."

"I haven't done it because of my mother's situation. Her health is in a dreadful decline. I'm not keen on having a constant stream of visitors through our house, which is what will certainly happen once the news is out."

"I am shocked that Lady Withnall hasn't found out yet and spread the gossip. Is she losing her touch? Getting soft in her old age?"

"I'm sure she knows. Nothing gets past her, but she and my mother were friends. If London's most prolific gossip has kept quiet about us, it is likely out of respect for her. Well, Lord Forster's ball is coming up soon. Everyone will know we've married as soon as his major-domo announces us. We'll be the talk of the party."

"Unless some other hapless bachelor happens to be caught with a sweet, young innocent in his arms. Then our news will immediately be forgotten for the latest scandal."

He chuckled. "Good, I've never liked being the center of everyone's attention. I look forward to being ignored and forgotten now that I am no longer a target for every matchmaking mother."

"Hopefully, no longer a target for Lady Sarah and her venom," she added, uncertain why the horrid debutante came into her mind at this moment. But she gave a little shiver, as though an ill wind had just shot through her despite the pleasantness of the day.

Tom appeared not to have felt it. "I cannot imagine why she should still care. I would not play along with her game. She ought to have gotten the hint by now that I will have nothing to do with her and her toady friends."

"You're right, of course." But why did this ill wind continue to whip around her? "Tom, let's go home."

CHAPTER SIXTEEN

HONEY GREETED ROSE and her husband, Julian Emory, whose official title was Viscount Chalmers, as they arrived for their quiet dinner party. Belle and Finn arrived shortly afterward. After exchanging pleasantries, they all sat down to dine.

Julian raised a glass in toast. "To the newlyweds," he said, his gaze on all four of them since Belle and Finn had only been married a month. "I wish you as happy as Rose and I."

They all cheered.

"You wanted to discuss your business," Rose said, opening the conversation they were all eager to have. "Striking the right balance is most important. Having husbands who don't feel threatened by your working and don't care what society thinks of it is crucial."

Honey looked at Tom, and her heart melted.

Intelligent eyes.

That's what she'd noticed about him right away. He was clever and confident and had wanted a wife who could keep up with him and not be a mere bauble on his arm.

He winked back at her.

She knew this discussion would go well.

"Decide what aspects of your business can only be done by you," Rose continued, "and choose wisely in delegating the rest."

"You also must be realistic in the ways your business can grow," Julian added. "Rose and I quickly realized we could not open our own shops or else we'd be forced to constantly travel all over England to oversee them. We have one factory with a shop attached to it near my estate and one warehouse in London. Our vendors come to us either at the warehouse or factory to purchase Rose's wares."

The discussion continued from the soup course, a simple leek soup, to their main courses, which consisted of smoked trout and apricot-glazed venison.

"It helps to have trusted family members to assist in overseeing not only the financial aspects but the design, manufacture, and distribution," Rose said between bites of trout. "There always seems to be pilfering going on, especially in the warehouse."

Julian set down his glass of wine and continued where Rose had left off. "We do our best to keep it to a minimum, but having someone in charge of security is a must. For this reason, we built our own factory. Easier to protect Rose's designs before they come out each season."

Rose grunted in disgust. "You'd be surprised how cutthroat this dinnerware business can be. Everyone is out to steal my newest glassware and dinnerware patterns. I'm sure it will be the same for your fragrances. I understand you had some nasty business in Oxford."

Belle nodded. "Yes, quite nasty. But Finn brought those horrid men to justice."

Finn laughed. "I needed the help of an entire regiment of soldiers. I hardly did it on my own."

Belle smiled at him. "You were brilliant."

"Says my completely impartial and obviously doting wife," Finn remarked, tossing her a steamy gaze.

The hour was late by the time the dinner party ended. After locking up the house for the night, Honey walked upstairs with Tom, liking the way he held her hand as they headed to their bedchamber. This seemed to be turning into a nightly ritual, closing up the house and then climbing the stairs together on their way to bed.

"It was a good discussion, don't you think?" she asked him.

"Yes, love. A very helpful one." When they reached the landing, she considered stopping in to see how Lady Wycke was doing but decided to put it off until the morning. Sadly, nothing had changed in the last three days. If anything, Tom's mother seemed to be retreating further and further into herself, no longer speaking or recognizing anyone.

Tom noticed the direction of her glance. "No, not tonight."

She reached up and kissed his cheek. "I love you."

He cast her a wicked grin. "Care to prove it?"

"You are incorrigible but also irresistible. Very well, you may have unimpeded access to my body. In turn, I shall cling to you all night." She shook her head, suddenly not feeling so cheerful. "I've had these odd feelings these past few days, as though someone is watching me."

She sighed and tried to shake off the thought. "Who would bother? The villains who tried to take over our Oxford shops are all in prison or confined elsewhere, pending their trials. I can't think of anyone else who'd care."

Tom frowned. "You are the most precious thing to me, Honey. Surely, you know this. How long precisely have you felt this?"

"The past three days."

"Finn mentioned a Bow Street runner he'd brought with him to Oxford."

"Homer Barrow. Yes, he's very good."

"I'll engage his services, have him follow you discreetly for the next week. If someone is watching you, he'll tell us who it is."

He surprised her by lifting her in his arms to carry her into their bedchamber. "There is another possible explanation for your unsettled feeling."

"What?"

"Do you think it's possible you are already with child? Lord knows, I haven't kept my hands off you, behaving like a rutting boar each night."

She shook her head and laughed. "First of all, your hands are not the problem. It's that other part of you that seems to like me very much. But I think it's too early for me to tell if I'm carrying your little viscount. In any event, it isn't my stomach that is feeling queasy. What I feel is more of a chill running up my spine."

He set her down on the bed and sat beside her. "Love, you must tell me right away if that feeling comes upon you again."

"I will."

He caressed her cheek. "And as for our nightly interludes, it doesn't matter that we're married. You can always tell me no. I won't be angry or ever force you."

"Perhaps that will happen when I'm the size of a whale and about to give birth. But I think we're perfect for now. Ask, and ye shall receive.' She smiled at him. "Come to bed, my love. My body is already aching for yours."

Their coupling was particularly sweet, but she sensed Tom was worried for her, and it made their joining all the more poignant. She worried that she'd added to his burdens by giving him yet another thing to fret about. However, it was the right decision.

Likely, it was nothing.

But if there was someone following her, she wanted Tom to put in place whatever was needed to protect her.

It was as much for his sake as for hers.

He loved her.

To have her injured would tear his heart to pieces.

That realization was brought home later the following day when she'd gone to visit his mother's bedchamber. She sat by her bed and took her hand. "Lady Wycke, how are you today?"

She was met with that same blank stare.

"His lordship was in here earlier today," Dora said with a sad shake of her head. "She's been like this too long now. She hardly eats. She won't move out of bed. She no longer speaks, not even to his lord-ship."

"I'll talk to my uncle about it when he comes by to see her." She nodded to Dora and Alice, who was serving as attendant for this day shift. "Thank you for keeping her as comfortable as possible."

She left a few minutes later and went in search of Tom. He wasn't in his study nor anywhere else in the main rooms of the house.

"Has he gone out, Winwood?" she asked their butler.

"No m'lady. I believe I saw him go upstairs a few minutes ago."

She nodded and hurried up the stairs, marching down the hall to their bedchamber. Her heart lurched the moment she stepped in and saw him seated on one of the wing chairs by the fireplace, his face buried in his hands. "Tom, my love."

She closed the door behind her and knelt at his side. "Talk to me about it."

He dropped his hands to his sides and looked at her, his expression revealing he was quite torn apart. "What is there to say? I used to hate it when she asked for me. *Tom. Where's my Tom? Ah, there you are. Where have you been?* I never knew whether she was looking for me or my father. Was she in the present or lost in the past? But now she says nothing at all, and it is so much worse."

"We'll talk to my Uncle George about it. He's due to visit her today."

He rubbed a hand across the nape of his neck. "He would have already done something if he could. I walked out of her bedchamber earlier because I wanted to rage and shake her and tell her to snap out of her stupor and talk to me. Even if she spoke gibberish, at least it would show she was here and not in some half-world between the living and the dead."

He groaned in anguish. "You're going to tell me I'm fighting na-ture again."

"You are, but it's all right. Perhaps I am too complacent, too quick to accept a situation and merely offer comfort instead of solutions."

He lifted her onto his lap. "No, my lady. You are quite perfect."

"So are you, my handsome lord." She offered no resistance when he kissed her deeply, his mouth covering hers with a possessive hunger. But she stopped him when he began to unlace her gown. "No, Tom! I have an appointment with Madame de Bressard for the final fitting on my gowns, and I cannot be late. Lord Forster's ball is tomorrow night, and her shop will be swarmed with ladies in panic for their gowns. If I'm even a few minutes late, I'll be struck off her list and won't be given an appointment with her for another month. She's more in demand than the queen herself. Come with me?"

He sighed but nodded. "Why not? I do need a bit of air."

Tom summoned his carriage, and they made it around the park and through the busy London streets with only minutes to spare by the time they drew up in front of the dressmaker's elegant shop. "You know, hers is a natural outlet for our soaps and perfumes. Once the season is officially over and all the lords have gone up to Scotland to hunt their grouse, I think I shall stop in and speak to her."

He nodded. "I'm not sure she'll have the space for your wares, but perhaps she'll set some aside, especially if she receives a percentage on your sales. It is easy earnings for her and not something that would compete with or detract from her dressmaking services."

"That's what I was thinking."

His good humor appeared to return, for he cast her a broad grin. "Our children will all be born wearing spectacles and carrying accounting ledgers."

She laughed. "I find nothing wrong with that."

They were quite merry as they walked into the shop until they ran into Lady Sarah and her two toady friends just walking out. "If it isn't Miss Farthingale and Lord Wycke. Or should I now refer to you as Lady Wycke? Don't the two of you make just the loveliest couple?" She laughed, although to Honey's ears, it sounded like a witch's cackle. Odious girl. "We shall see how long your wedded bliss lasts. Looking forward to seeing you at Lord Forster's ball. You will attend, will you not? I wouldn't want you to miss the fun."

She knocked past them, but her friends skittered around them, too daunted by Tom's dark scowl.

Honey shook her head and sighed. "Sorry, Tom. You didn't need her piling on to the woes of your already miserable day."

He kissed her cheek. "My concern was for you. She is nothing to me, and there is nothing she can ever say or do to hurt me."

Honey merely smiled at him, but the chill had just run up her spine again.

Why had Lady Sarah mentioned Lord Forster's ball? It might have been innocent. After all, the ball was tomorrow evening. But Honey sensed it was something more.

What was the horrid girl planning?

CHAPTER SEVENTEEN

Tom DIDN'T THINK he could be prouder than to escort Honey to Lord Forster's ball. He studied her in fascination as she gave a merry twirl to show off her gown. "Do I make a worthy countess? What do you think of the gold silk? Isn't it beautiful? I love the fiery sheen to it. When I dance, the gown will appear to change in hue depending on the way the candlelight strikes it. Of course, this is one of Uncle John's fabrics. I'm sure Uncle Rupert or my cousin, William, came back with it from one of their trips along the Silk Road."

Tom folded his arms across his chest. "It's beautiful, and you are exquisite. An irresistible temptation, quite golden and sweet."

"Like one of those sticky hot cross buns?" She rolled her eyes. "You are grinning at me like a hyena."

"I can't help it. I find you charming. Don't berate me for adoring my wife." He caught her in his arms. "You'll be the prettiest lady there. Were you still unattached, you'd have a line of beaus out the door. I'd have to chase them all off, of course."

"How tiresome for you." But she laughed. "I see how it is. You only married me to save yourself the bother of chasing away your rivals."

"There are several other benefits to marrying you." He kissed her soundly on the lips but held back from ravishing her as he wished. She looked beautiful. Happy. Excited. Dimples formed in her cheeks whenever she smiled broadly, as she was doing now. Her eyes were sparkling, that incredible, shimmering blue. "Come along, my love. Time to make your first formal appearance as my countess."

She also wore the Wycke diamond and ruby necklace. He'd given it to her earlier to wear as a complement to her gown. The diamonds shimmered at her slender throat. The necklace was only permitted to be worn by Honey since she was the present countess. Not even his mother could wear it now that he'd taken her as his bride.

Not that his mother would have an inkling about the family's heirloom jewels.

Did she even know who she was?

He suppressed the dark thoughts bubbling just beneath his calm facade. Nothing to be done for this loving woman who'd raised him. He could only arrange to keep her comfortable and visit her every day in the hope there was a glimmer of her former self still lurking inside her aging shell.

Honey was so finely attuned to him.

She gave his hand a light squeeze. "You look magnificent, my lord. But I have a problem."

He immediately took notice. "What is it, my love?"

"My dance card is woefully empty. I need someone to fill it."

"Ah, a weighty problem indeed." He tucked her arm in his to escort her downstairs to their waiting carriage. "Need I point out that you don't have a dance card yet, nor will you need one since you already know I'm a possessive arse, and no one is going to fill it but me."

"Actually, you have a rather nice, firm ar–" She blushed furiously, the comment she was about to make dying on her lips when she noticed Winwood standing at the foot of the stairs with her gloves in his hand.

He'd obviously overheard her remark, although he did a commendable job of maintaining a stony expression.

"Ah, Winwood. Thank you. Lady Wycke was wondering where

her gloves had gone to."

Tom grinned at her once they were settled in the carriage. "You're still blushing."

She shook her head and groaned. "What your butler must think of me!"

"Why? Because you almost passed a comment about my arse? I can assure you, he's probably heard worse. Not just us talking, either. His room is immediately above our bedchamber. Not to mention, Merrick's room is just next door."

"Your valet, too?" Her face was on fire. "How much do you think they heard?"

"Of us in bed?" He chuckled. "All of it. You are noisy in your passion."

"Oh, Tom!"

"Gad, you're too easy to tease. Of course, they haven't heard us. The bedroom walls are far too thick." *I hope.*

She lightly kicked his shin. "You are a terrible man. My heart is in palpitations."

He shifted over to sit beside her instead of across from her. "Perhaps I ought to check it out. Let me put an ear to it."

"Naughty creature." But she was laughing merrily. "You've just stuck your nose in my cleavage. And that is your hand, not your ear. And that is my breast, not my heart." She was still laughing as she pushed him back into the seat across from her. "I will not have you drooling worse than Jasper all over the front of my gown. No wonder they called you Wicked Wycke."

He continued to tease her but far more gently. He liked that she gave back as good as she got. Her quick wit and playfulness always put him back in good humor. He also liked her innocent charm, her gullibility despite her obvious intelligence.

It was refreshing.

He helped her down from their carriage when they arrived at Lord

Forster's elegant London mansion. They waited in line to greet their host and be announced.

Gasps filled the air, and all eyes in the ballroom turned to them the moment the major-domo announced them. "Lord Wycke and Lady Wycke."

Silence surrounded them for several heartbeats, then the room erupted in chatter as everyone began to move toward them. They were surrounded by well-wishers. Some others held back, mostly those who had held hope their daughters might make a match with him. The sight of Honey wearing the Wycke necklace dashed their plans.

Also hanging back with a malicious smile on her lips was Lady Sarah.

Hell and damnation.

He'd hired Homer Barrow to follow Honey around, but the man had noticed nothing out of the ordinary. Was it possible Sarah had already discovered whatever it was she was hoping to find to hurt Honey and no longer needed to shadow her?

Or was he blowing everything out of proportion and giving the wretched girl more credit than she deserved?

When the crowd finally parted and they'd made their way across the ballroom, Lady Sarah gave a shout to gain everyone's attention. She stood on the steps they'd just descended to enter the ballroom and held a glass of champagne in her hands. She raised it high, as though to offer them a toast. "Cheers, Lord Wycke. May your happiness be dashed. You may think you've got yourself the perfect bride. A perfect lady. But she has a secret, one I'm sure she has not shared with you. And now I shall tell you and all the world."

"Tom, no!" Honey held him back as he started toward Sarah, knowing he could not reach the witch in time to shut her up, but he didn't care.

He wanted to snap her neck.

Finn and his brothers blocked his way, obviously fearing he meant to murder the duke's daughter. Indeed, this is what he would have done were she a man. But she was a female viper, so all he could really do was carry her out of everyone's hearing.

"Let me go, Finn," he growled, trying to shrug out of his grip.

"Not until you calm down."

"I am calm." More Braydens put their hands on him to restrain him. He managed to toss off three, but by that time, another three had come forward. He himself was big, but so were these Brayden men. Big as damn oxen. He was no match for all of them.

"You are now trapped in marriage to a bastard," Lady Sarah taunted as he struggled to break free and silence the banshee. "She lied to you. She is no genteel lady but an illegitimate, baseborn nobody. Have I shocked you, Lord Wycke? The lady you've chosen to wear your precious heirloom necklace was born out of wedlock. Isn't that rich? What a taint to your proud and noble bloodline."

Her toady friends now stood beside her, their champagne flutes raised in triumph.

Tom felt such a deep ache for the humiliation poured on Honey, but the damage was done, and he now had to undo it. Were she a man, she would not have lived to take another breath.

But as detestable as she was, he could not strike her.

Even at the height of his rage, he would not have hurt her. It simply wasn't in him to ever beat a woman. All he meant to do was drag her out of the room and call her father into Lord Forster's study to deal with her outrageous behavior.

But she'd gone too far in her attempt to destroy Honey to make the matter private now. He finally shrugged out of Finn's grasp. Honey had moved toward him and now stood by his side. He put his arm around her, a trembling rage flowing through him.

He had yet to calm when he turned to Lady Sarah. "I am only shocked by your stupidity and saddened by how tragically pathetic your life must be to spend your time obsessing over how to destroy the happiness of another. My wife has never lied to me. *Never.* There is nothing you can say, no malicious gossip you can ever spread to shake my faith in her or my love for her. She is a lady through and through, and I am proud to have her wear my family's heirloom jewels. She honors me by accepting to be my wife. As for you, is this the life you've made for yourself? Unhappy, angry, jealous. You are the laughingstock, and so are the peahens you believe are your friends."

"My father will call you out for this!"

"I doubt it."

"Your wife is a–"

Her father came up from behind her and dragged her toward him and Honey. "Get on bended knee and apologize to Lord and Lady Wycke at once," he said, his voice and body shaking with unbridled fury. "My abject apologies Lady Wycke." He then turned back to his daughter. "Get on your knees."

"No, please." Honey grabbed hold of Tom's arm as she spoke, obviously needing the support, although there might also have been a desire to hold him back, for he was still enraged. As Nathaniel had said, these Farthingales had finesse and knew how to handle two problems at once.

Surprisingly, Honey's touch calmed him. He still wanted to wring Sarah's neck but had regained enough of his control to know he would not do her physical harm, no matter how much she provoked him.

"Please, Your Grace," Honey said, her voice gentle. "It isn't necessary. I do not want her to kneel before me. She is not well. This is too much humiliation for her to bear."

The Duke of Remson appeared about to cry. "Wycke, your wife has more honor in her little finger than my daughter will ever have in her entire body. If there is anything to know of Lady Wycke's past, it is obvious you know it already, for she is not the sort to ever connive or lie to you. Even now, she has shown my undeserving daughter nothing but compassion. You have married a jewel."

He turned away and dragged his daughter out of the ballroom.

Her friends scurried after her like the brainless peahens they were.

No one moved or said anything for the longest time. Then the crowd parted as Lord Forster and his wife made their way toward him and Honey. "It is my custom to open the ball by dancing with my wife. However, she has advised me that she'd rather be escorted around the dance floor by a handsome man and not an old goat of a husband."

Tom grinned.

"Would you do me the honor of opening the ball by partnering with my wife? And I shall be delighted to partner with Lady Wycke."

The gesture was enormously kind, and Tom told Lady Forster so as he twirled her about the dance floor. "I must also give my apologies for the scene caused."

"Nonsense, Wycke. You and your lovely wife have made our ball a success. It will be all anyone talks about until next year's ball. You have added to our cachet."

He glanced over at Honey, trying to keep his eyes on her as others now came onto the dance floor to join in this opening waltz.

"Worried about your wife?"

He nodded.

"She's made of stern stuff. I suppose it's true. She's illegitimate. These outrageous accusations often are. But what matters most is that you knew it already. I suppose your wife told you before you married her."

Tom hesitated to respond, but the damn secret was out, and he was relieved, more for Honey's sake than for his own. He loved her too much. The circumstances of her birth were inconsequential to him. The sooner it all came to light, the sooner everyone would forget about the supposedly shameful secret. "Yes, she told me everything before accepting my proposal. She wouldn't marry me until I had time to consider the truth."

"Then she is, as you said, a lady through and through."

"Thank you, Lady Forster. Indeed, she is."

"I was an opera singer when my husband met me."

Tom laughed.

"I mention it because I see how you worry for her. But you mustn't. It will all be forgotten in a few years, likely sooner. But, ah me. I am so sorry for His Grace and that daughter of his. I suppose he'll ship her off to one of his estates in Scotland now. The girl will never step foot in London while he is alive."

"She will not be missed."

"No, the nasty ones never are. Life is difficult enough. Who needs that sort of filth piled up on it?"

The rest of the ball passed smoothly. Tom returned to Honey's side and danced the next two dances with her, more for his need to touch her and know she was all right. "I will be fine, my love."

"Are you certain? I'm so sorry this happened. She likely was following you around London, desperate to find a way to destroy you."

"She hasn't hurt me, as you can see. But Tom, you must stop looking at me in that besotted way or all your bachelor friends will be making fun of you."

He laughed. "Let them."

A moment later, he sobered. "What Lord and Lady Forster did for us was quite gracious. There may be others who are less accepting and will give you the cut."

"I know. They were never my friends, nor shall I miss them. Nor will I care. I have you and a very large, extended family, and hope to count the Forsters among our friends. It is all the company I need."

He offered to dance a third with Honey. "Oh, no. I've had quite enough of you, my exceedingly handsome and overly protective lord. Go. I know how much you enjoy your game of cards. Don't let me hold you back."

He sighed. "I can skip it."

"No, your normal routine is important. I'll sit with Hortensia and my cousins. I'll be quite happy and safe with them."

Reluctantly, he joined Finn and his brothers in the card room. He and Finn often played cards together, so they'd known each other fairly well before becoming brothers-in-law. "I wasn't really going to strangle Lady Sarah," he grumbled, catching Finn frowning at him. "You needn't have stopped me."

"You were mad enough to take down three Braydens before we subdued you. I don't think anyone has ever managed that feat before. But you are family now. We protect our own, even from themselves when necessary."

"Duly noted." He dealt the cards, and they played several rounds until the dinner bell rang. He and Finn rose, for it was time to escort their wives to the dining hall. "How is Belle? I should have asked sooner. I'm sure the scene she witnessed was most upsetting to her. I'm glad that demented harpy left Belle alone."

"Belle was concerned, of course. How could she not be distraught to see her sister attacked? But Honey showed poise under fire."

"And I behaved like a flaming arse." Tom shook his head. "I would have killed her if she were a man."

"I know."

"But she's a female. I'm not sure what I would have done to shut her up. Maybe tossed her over my knee and spanked her. Well, that's hitting. I couldn't have done that. Perhaps carried her out and dumped her in the street. Probably couldn't have done that either."

Finn shook his head. "That girl is going to come across someone who will have no such reservations. She had better learn to curb her spiteful tongue."

"Honey is worried that her father will beat her. But he won't. If he were the sort, he would have done it long ago. She certainly gave him enough cause."

The conversation was dropped as they met their wives.

Later that night, once they were home and in bed, Tom took Honey in his arms. "Are you truly all right, love?"

She nodded. "I think so. Are you?"

"Not quite yet, but I'll get past it. She tried to destroy you."

"And you think you are somehow to blame?" She kissed him lightly on the jaw, no doubt feeling his tension against her lips. "She is the one who did this, not you."

"I should have done something to prevent it."

"There is nothing you could have done. She was determined to destroy my reputation and our marriage. She's failed at both. I'm relieved she was merely waving a champagne glass while ranting and not a pistol. Then someone really might have been hurt. But you are still wound in a tight coil." She ran her hand along his arm to soothe him. "Your muscle is still hard as a rock. Why are you so troubled, Tom?"

"I don't know."

"Yes, you do." She kissed him again. "Shall we talk about your feelings?"

"Bollocks, no."

"Because I think what has you clenching your hands and grinding your teeth is the feeling of helplessness. You couldn't stop Lady Sarah from trying to ruin me, just as you can't stop your mother's failing health."

"Can we not speak of this in bed?"

"The ironic thing about it all is that the biggest scandal is yet to be."

He frowned. "What do you mean?"

"Society will be unforgiving of a countess in trade. That I will continue to help my family run our perfume business will offend the Upper Crust more than the circumstances of my birth. Do you think you are up to facing that scandal?"

He emitted a groaning laugh. "Yes, I'm up for it. I should have realized..."

"Realized what, my love?"

He shifted her under him and began to trail kisses along her neck. "I should have realized when marrying a Farthingale, my life will never be complacent or sedentary again."

She cupped his face and frowned in response to his words. "I'm so sorry, Tom. I'll try my best to—"

"To what? Be a good and biddable wife? No, love. You think for yourself. You don't blindly follow what some else tells you to do. You are far too independent for that. The words meek, docile, and obedient are not in the Farthingale vocabulary."

"Of course, they are...sometimes...often."

"Rarely. But I don't mind. That's not why I married you. And while I obviously adore and worship your body," he said, now kissing his way along her sweet, warm skin, tasting her and loving the way she responded to the touch of his hands and lips. "I married you because you will always challenge me to be the best man I can be. You will always calm me when I want to roar in frustration. You will always give me hope, show me the beauty and promise in life. This is why I love you. This is why I shall remain deeply and irrevocably in love with you for the rest of my days."

"That was a lovely speech, but I have a confession to make."

He stopped kissing her and propped up on one elbow. "What is it, love?"

"I only married you for your body."

He burst out laughing.

But this is how their marriage would always be, for Honey added smiles and lightness to his being.

He settled over her, loving the way she was always soft and willing. "Have at my body to your heart's desire, my impertinent countess."

"Thank you, my lord. I shall do just that."

CHAPTER EIGHTEEN

London, England
October 1820

HONEY STOOD IN the bedchamber she shared with Tom, peering out the window. It was still quite early in the morning, but they were up and dressed, preparing to head downstairs to join his newly arrived sister and her husband for breakfast. "What are you doing, Tom? I'm usually the one who is always slow to get ready."

"Just organizing some documents to give to Anne. I'm sure Malcolm will want to look them over while they're here."

The sky was an overcast gray, and a strong north wind was doing an efficient job of blowing the last few leaves off the trees in their garden. Honey watched them being tossed in the air, their golds and deep reds catching her eye as they floated for several moments before dropping to the hard ground beside the rose trellis.

Only a few red roses remained in bloom, their vibrant petals, a crimson in color, quite beautiful against the dying foliage.

Tom came to stand behind her, wrapping her in his arms and drawing her up against his chest. "You remind me of those red roses. The fiery tinge to your hair. Your stunning beauty. Your resilience. The softness of your petals." He nuzzled her neck.

"I don't have petals. Perhaps a few thorns."

"No, you're perfect."

She laughed and turned in his arms to face him. "Lord Wycke, my wicked and wonderful lord. You must not flatter me as we are about to leave our bedchamber, or I shall drag you back to bed and never let you out of it. We shall get nothing done. Ever. The house will fall to ruin. The roof will collapse about our heads. The servants will run off. Our situation will be quite dire."

"All because of an extra hour in bed? Amazing." He planted a loud, wet kiss on her cheek. "Then I had better get you out of here."

As they headed to the door, ridiculously slow because they weren't quite finished kissing each other, they heard a sudden banging on their door. "Tom! Are you in there? Come quickly."

His sister was urgently summoning him.

He threw open the door. "What is it, Anne?"

"It's our mother. She's opened her eyes. She's calling for you."

Honey entwined her fingers in his as they hurried down the hall. She knew what was going through his mind, feeling hope one moment and dread in the next. His stomach had to be twisted in knots.

Anne scurried ahead of them. "'Where's Tom? Where's my Tom?' That's what she's been saying over and over."

"She isn't asking for me, Anne. She's calling for our father."

"I don't know. It feels like she's asking for you, Tom."

"Well, here we are. Let's see." The three of them hurried in, but Honey held back to allow him and his sister some privacy as they sat close to their mother's bed.

Lady Wycke's aged, reddened eyes settled on her son. "Tom, there you are. Where have you been?"

"I'm here now, my darling." He took her hand in both of his.

She gazed at Honey. "Oh, my dear. I'm so glad you've come, too." She waved Honey closer.

At Tom's nod, she moved to stand beside him, resting a hand lightly on his shoulder.

"Anne, where's your big hulk of a husband?"

Anne grinned. "Eating, of course. How else is he to maintain his muscled magnificence?"

Lady Wycke chuckled. "He's a good man. I'm glad you're so happy, my beautiful girl."

Anne burst into tears. "I am, Mama. I'll fetch Malcolm. He'll want to give you a kiss now that you're awake."

Honey sank into the chair she had just vacated. "And dear, Honey. You and Poppy were so sweet to me at our country party. My son is wild for you. I've never seen him look at another girl the way he looks at you. Has he proposed to you yet?"

Honey was going to burst into tears as well. "He has, Lady Wycke."

"And you've accepted? I'm sure you must have. He's irresistible."

Tom let out a genuinely mirthful laugh. "Gad, that's a mother talking if I ever heard one."

"He is irresistible," Honey said with a nod. "He has completely stolen my heart."

"As Honey has stolen mine. I've married her. She is my wife. For a little over a month now." He was still holding his mother's hand. "I'm sorry, my darling. You were too ill to attend. We tried to tell you afterward…"

"I heard you. But I've not been myself. I thought I might have dreamed it. Well, it doesn't matter, dearest. I know now. All I've ever wanted was for you to be happy, and I can see you are. Thank goodness both my children chose well. I'm so tired, Tom."

Honey saw tears forming in his eyes.

"So very tired. Your father is waiting for me. I think it won't be long now."

Anne returned with her husband. "No, Mama!"

"Oh, my dear Anne. You've brought your Malcolm. Give us a kiss, you naughty boy. Stealing my daughter's heart in an afternoon."

Malcolm grinned. "Och, yer daughter is the one who led me astray. Captured my heart at first glance. What else could I do but marry her?"

"Tell me about the children?"

She and Tom left his sister and her husband chatting with her and went downstairs to have their breakfast, although Honey doubted either of them would eat much. But her stomach growled the moment she saw the chafing dishes neatly lined up on the buffet and immediately went over to them.

"Do you believe in miracles, Tom?" she asked, piling kippers, eggs, and sausages onto her plate. Well, perhaps she was hungrier than she realized.

"No, love." He stood beside her, watching her fill the plate. "You sure you can eat all that?"

She nodded. "But your mother is awake and talking, recognizing her children. I feared she might never be alert again. Perhaps hearing Anne's voice stirred her. How can it not be a miracle?"

When they sat, he at the head of the table and she beside him, he took her hand in his and gave it an affectionate squeeze. "Perhaps it *is* Anne's voice that has her opening her eyes. They were always very close. She and Malcolm wanted her to come live with them. But the weather is harsh that far north, and her life has always been here. Besides," he said with a wry grin, "she probably thought she needed to keep an eye on her wayward son."

"I know you would have remained as wise and good as you always have been. I would have fallen deeply in love with you with or without your mother around to curb your wicked ways."

"Ah, spoken like a doting wife." His gaze was warm and tender. "I doubt her improvement will be permanent. For all we know, she may have said all she needed to say to Anne and me, and already be slipping back into her other world. How long before she calls out to me again, thinking I'm my father? 'Where's my Tom? There you are, my Tom. Where have you been?'"

"It doesn't matter. We shall love her and be grateful for those moments she is with us." She speared an entire kipper and stuffed it in her mouth.

He stared at her.

"What?"

"Nothing." He shook his head. "It won't tear me up anymore to hear her say it. I think the worst for me has been not hearing her speak at all, watching her drift so far into herself, she can no longer see or hear us."

"Let's just take it one day at a time, my love." She speared another kipper and stuffed it in her mouth. Followed by a forkful of eggs. She swallowed all of it down quickly. "No matter what happens, she doesn't want us to cry over her. We will, of course. But not today. This is a good day. She is back with us for now. Your sister is here and so full of love for you. I shall plan a party for her before she and Malcolm return to Scotland."

He nodded. "She'll enjoy meeting your family. I believe she knows Violet and Poppy already."

Honey set down her fork and cleared her throat. "I have another reason to rejoice."

He placed his elbows on the table and watched her intently. "What reason might that be?"

She cleared her throat again. "A very good reason. I'm fairly certain. Although I'm not completely sure. But I think it must be." She took a deep breath. "We may have a little viscount on the way."

"A baby?" Tom looked upon her with such love, he simply melted her heart.

Anne and Malcolm happened to walk in just as Tom drew her out of her chair and kissed her so thoroughly, even the big Scot blushed.

"Don't go," Tom said, calling them back when they meant to leave them to their private interlude. "There's a reason I am kissing my wife. Anne, can you believe it? I'm going to be a father."

Then all of them were around her, hugging and congratulating her. "I told you, didn't I, Malcolm? One look at you, Honey, and I knew. Yes, you are. Let me remove any doubt you might have. You are indeed carrying a little viscount."

Tom took her in his arms and kissed her again.

"Well, we'll leave you to it," Anne said, tucking her arm in Malcolm's and hurrying him out.

Honey smiled at her husband. "It was probably not the right moment to tell you, but—"

"It was the perfect moment. A new life brought into our family. I love you, Honey."

"I love you, too. Shall we run upstairs and tell your mother?"

"Give me a moment. Let me enjoy having you to myself."

She laughed. "You have such a grin on your face."

"You have a way of making me smile whenever I'm with you. It's a Farthingale trait, I think. That ability to turn their husbands into besotted, grinning fools. Whenever one is in the presence of a Farthingale, it is only a matter of time before happy chaos and mayhem ensues."

"That is completely untrue."

"Utterly true." He looked over her head to the entrance. "Winwood?"

"Mrs. Violet Brayden is here to see her cousin. Urgently."

Honey's eyes widened in surprise. "Yes, please. Do have her come in."

Violet burst in a moment later and threw her arms around Honey. "There is something important I must ask you."

"Of course. What is it?" She glanced at Tom and shrugged.

"Did you give *The Book of Love* to Holly?"

"Yes, just yesterday morning. She's been dodging me for weeks now, but I finally got it into her hands. Why?"

"Oh, that explains it." She looked at Tom in dismay. "Lord Wycke, you cannot repeat a word of what I am about to tell you. Please, do I have your promise?"

"Yes," Tom said, eyeing her curiously.

Violet took Honey's hands in hers. "You must not breathe a word of it either, Honey."

"My lips are sealed. What is the matter?"

"I was sure you had passed the book off to her…and this cannot be mentioned to anyone else. Not anyone. Not her sisters. Or the family elders, good heavens, not them. Nor the cousins."

"For goodness sake, Violet. Just come out with it."

"Holly caught Joshua Brayden standing naked in my kitchen last night. I mean…*naked*. Not a stitch on him. Not even a scrap of cloth to cover…you know, those parts."

Tom burst out laughing. "What did I tell you, Honey?"

She rolled her eyes. "What was Holly doing in your house? For that matter, why was Joshua there in the first place? And what happened to his clothes?"

"It is all quite innocent."

Tom shook his head, still laughing. "Of course, it is. It's always innocent with you Farthingales. Have a seat, Violet. Have you had your breakfast?"

"I've eaten, thank you." But she sat beside Honey and stared at the pile of food on her plate. "You're awfully hungry this morning."

"We were talking about Joshua's missing clothes. What happened?"

Violet leaned closer, her voice barely above a whisper. "I was next door with the family to celebrate Hortensia's birthday. Joshua had just come back from an assignment. He was exhausted and dirty after ten days of hard riding. He thought the house was empty because I was supposed to leave for Plymouth several days ago to meet Romulus, and it was arranged that he would stay in our house until I returned."

Tom was still casting her that smug, I-told-you-so look. "But your plans changed."

"Yes. However, we had no way of getting word to Joshua. Well, it is of no importance now. I've been sleeping over at Uncle John's anyway, sharing a room with Holly. Which is why she knew I would not be in my own home when she crept in last night and tried to hide *The Book of Love* in one of my bureau drawers."

"That still doesn't explain Joshua's missing clothes," Tom reminded them.

"He was taking a bath to wash off the dust and grime of the road. Since he did not wish to disturb the servants, he went into the kitchen, dragged the tub from the corner where it is stored, and set it in front of the large cooking hearth. He set a fire, boiled water, and filled the tub."

Tom chuckled. "Quite enterprising of him."

Honey frowned.

"He'd just finished bathing when Holly walked in. Well, timing is everything, isn't it?"

Honey groaned. "Oh, no."

"Oh, yes. He had just gotten out of the tub, and there she was. And there he was. All of him. He stood beside the hearth with his altogether hanging out. She stood by the door. Unimpeded view of him. His drying cloth was across the kitchen, atop one of the tables."

Tom snorted. "Lord, you can't make this up."

Violet shook her head. "You mustn't breathe a word of this to anyone. Holly doesn't even know that I know. Joshua told me. Not that he wanted to, but he thought Holly might have said something to me, and he wanted to assure me he was a gentleman. I never had any doubt. Braydens are ridiculously honorable."

She gave Honey a quick hug and glanced at her plate again. "Why are you eating enough to choke a horse? And Tom hasn't stopped grinning since I walked in. I know that grin. Nathaniel wore that same grin when Poppy told him…" She shrieked and ran off.

Honey shot to her feet. "Violet, wait!"

"I'll be back later with the others," her cousin shouted from the hall, still chattering as she tore out of the house. "Congratulations!"

Honey wasn't certain what to say to Tom. He had the oddest look on his face. Finally, he laughed and took her in his arms. "I love you more than words can say, Honey."

"Oh, Tom. Even after that? What did you call it? Chaos and mayhem? And on such a day."

"It is especially appreciated on such a day. This is how my parents hoped my life would turn out. My mother is an artist. A free spirit. You did not know her in her prime. She would have adored all your relatives. She'll be delighted when we tell her. Even if she has retreated into her shell. There's a part of her that will know and rejoice for us. A family of our own," he said, placing a hand on her stomach. "Friends and relatives popping in at all hours. A house filled with children and barking dogs. Give me a kiss, my beautiful Lady Wycke. I think this might be the best day of my life."

She kissed him sweetly on the lips.

A kiss of pure happiness.

A kiss of love.

Also by Meara Platt

About the Author

Meara Platt is a USA Today bestselling author and an award winning, Amazon UK All-star. Her favorite place in all the world is England's Lake District, which may not come as a surprise since many of her stories are set in that idyllic landscape, including her award-winning paranormal romance Dark Gardens series. If you'd like to learn more about the ancient Fae prophecy that is about to unfold in the Dark Gardens series, as well as Meara's lighthearted, international bestselling Regency romances in the Farthingale series, Book of Love series, and the Braydens series, please visit Meara's website at www.mearaplatt.com.

Made in the USA
Columbia, SC
07 March 2025

54837717R00120